From the files of Kelly Chapman

JANE HAMILTON. First wife of murder suspect
and bigamist. Well-regarded magazine editor.
Close friends with Bradley Manchester—who wants
to move their relationship to a deeper level.
Jane is resisting. But unless she confronts the past—
with honesty—she won't attain happiness
in the present....

Praise for the novels of Tara Taylor Quinn

"One of the skills that has served Quinn best...
has been her ability to explore edgier subjects."
Publishers Weekly

"Combining her usual superb sense of
characterization with a realistically gritty plot,
Quinn has created an exceptionally powerful book."
—*Booklist* on *Behind Closed Doors*

"I thoroughly enjoyed [*Behind Closed Doors*] to the
point where I could not put it down to attend to such
routine things as eating. I was riveted from the first
page to the last."
—*All About Romance*

"Tara Taylor Quinn has created a masterpiece with
The Night We Met.... This novel deserves to sit on
every reader's shelf as a keeper. I highly recommend
all readers of women's fiction, romance and series
grab their copies today and prepare to be taken for
the emotional ride of their life."
—*Love Romances and More*

"Lisa Jackson fans will fall hard for Quinn's
unique ability to explore edgy subjects
with mesmerizing style."
—*BookReporter.com*

Dear Reader,

Welcome! You're about to get details from the first of many private files of psychologist and expert witness Kelly Chapman. This character first presented herself to me a couple of years ago, and I'm excited to share her life and her files with you.

Kelly is in demand all over the country, but she's lived in the same town, Chandler, Ohio, most of her life. She has also counseled many of the citizens of Chandler, so while she is loved by many, intimate personal relationships are kind of out for her. At home she's happily ruled by her four-pound toy poodle, Princess Camille, who allows Kelly to address her as Camy.

The First Wife is the story of Jane Hamilton, a successful magazine editor who's on top of her game until she finds out that not only has she been lied to in the most hideous way, but she's also been lying to herself. She's called to testify at a trial. The defendant is her ex-husband. The crime—he's been accused of murdering his wife. Jane is the *first* wife. Complications arise from the fact that Jane's husband was a bigamist—married to the woman he murdered at the same time he was married to Jane. And there's a third wife, too. But the complications don't end there. Don't worry, though. Jane does find love again. And you'll learn what happened during Jane's first marriage and afterward. Kelly Chapman takes great notes!

For access to more of Kelly's files, check out these upcoming MIRA releases in THE CHAPMAN FILES— *The Second Lie* (October 2010), *The Third Secret* (November 2010) and *The Fourth Victim* (December 2010).

I love hearing from readers. You can reach me at P.O. Box 13584, Mesa, Arizona 85216, or through my Web site, www.tarataylorquinn.com.

Tara Taylor Quinn

TARA TAYLOR QUINN

The First Wife

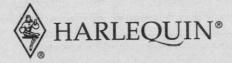

TORONTO • NEW YORK • LONDON
AMSTERDAM • PARIS • SYDNEY • HAMBURG
STOCKHOLM • ATHENS • TOKYO • MILAN • MADRID
PRAGUE • WARSAW • BUDAPEST • AUCKLAND

Recycling programs
for this product may
not exist in your area.

ISBN-13: 978-0-373-71656-2

THE FIRST WIFE

Copyright © 2010 by Tara Taylor Quinn.

All rights reserved. Except for use in any review, the reproduction or utilization of this work in whole or in part in any form by any electronic, mechanical or other means, now known or hereafter invented, including xerography, photocopying and recording, or in any information storage or retrieval system, is forbidden without the written permission of the publisher, Harlequin Enterprises Limited, 225 Duncan Mill Road, Don Mills, Ontario, Canada M3B 3K9.

This is a work of fiction. Names, characters, places and incidents are either the product of the author's imagination or are used fictitiously, and any resemblance to actual persons, living or dead, business establishments, events or locales is entirely coincidental.

This edition published by arrangement with Harlequin Books S.A.

For questions and comments about the quality of this book please contact us at Customer_eCare@Harlequin.ca.

® and TM are trademarks of the publisher. Trademarks indicated with ® are registered in the United States Patent and Trademark Office, the Canadian Trade Marks Office and in other countries.

www.eHarlequin.com

Printed in U.S.A.

ABOUT THE AUTHOR

The author of more than fifty original novels published in twenty languages, Tara Taylor Quinn is a *USA TODAY* bestselling writer with over six million copies sold. She is known for her deeply emotional and psychologically astute novels. Tara won a 2008 Readers' Choice Award, is a four-time finalist for the prestigious RWA RITA® Award, a multiple finalist for the Reviewers' Choice Award, the Booksellers' Best Award and the Holt Medallion, among others. She has appeared on national and local TV across the country, including CBS *Sunday Morning.* When she's not writing or fulfilling speaking engagements, Tara loves to travel with her husband, stopping wherever the spirit takes them. Home is in Ohio, where they live with their two dogs.

Books by Tara Taylor Quinn

HARLEQUIN SUPERROMANCE

1309—THE PROMISE
     OF CHRISTMAS
1350—A CHILD'S WISH
1381—MERRY CHRISTMAS,
     BABIES
1428—SARA'S SON
1446—THE BABY GAMBLE
1465—THE VALENTINE GIFT
     "Valentine's Daughters"
1500—TRUSTING RYAN
1527—THE HOLIDAY VISITOR
1550—SOPHIE'S SECRET*
1584—A DAUGHTER'S TRUST

HARLEQUIN SINGLE TITLE

SHELTERED IN HIS ARMS*

*Shelter Valley Stories

MIRA BOOKS

WHERE THE ROAD ENDS
STREET SMART
HIDDEN
IN PLAIN SIGHT
BEHIND CLOSED DOORS
AT CLOSE RANGE

HARLEQUIN EVERLASTING LOVE

THE NIGHT WE MET

For Tim. My first and last. I love you, babe.

PROLOGUE

Saturday, March 20, 2010
Chandler, Ohio

I WAS SITTING at my kitchen table that morning, having a banana and trying to decide whether to skate first—I'm an avid in-line skater—or read a couple of patient files and then skate, when the phone rang.

Not all that unusual. I'd lived in Chandler my entire life—except for when I was in college. I was on the committee to beautify Main Street, volunteered at our version of a soup kitchen, belonged to a book club, mentored a doctoral candidate for State Board of Psychology Licensure. And any number of my clients had my home phone number. I lived in a small town. There was no escaping them.

And truth be told, I didn't want to escape them. I wanted to help them. I cared about them. Regardless of what the professors had taught us in all of my Clinical Psychology classes—that we were not to personalize our work—I got emotionally involved with my patients' care. My professors' theories worked on an academic level. They didn't work in Chandler. Bottom line was, trauma didn't punch a time clock. So neither did I. But I digress.

I was going to read files. Two in particular. And I was

going to skate. The only question was which I would do first.

And then the call came.

Camy, or Camelia as the royal queen of the four-pound toy poodle world is more formally known, jumped down from my lap as I grabbed the phone.

I recognized the number on the display. Sheila Grant was one of Ohio's leading county prosecutors. She also happened to live in Chandler—probably because, as the seat of Ford County, Chandler has the only courthouse.

A few years older than me, Sheila had been at her job a long time. And with her lover, Geraldine, even longer. I respected her. Liked her, even, but we'd never been close. Sheila enjoyed motorcycles, demolition derbies and pig roasts.

I didn't.

"Hello?" That was the way I always answered the phone. Didn't matter that now, with caller ID, I knew who was on the other end. I mean, what if it was my dad's number and I let out a "what do you want?" and it turned out to be a cop using my dad's phone to call and tell me Dad was dead on the side of the road?

"Good, you're there," Sheila said, her voice as feminine as her skin was tough.

"Yep. For the moment. What's up?"

"I have a case."

Of course she did. It was the only reason the prosecutor would be calling me at home. If she was selling raffle tickets for her latest cause, she'd have caught me at the courthouse. Or my office.

"What kind of case?"

"It's a strange one, Kel," Sheila said. "Murder, but that's not what's weird."

"Okay." I grabbed the pen and pad of paper from the counter because it was closer than the one on the table. Or the one beside the couch. Besides, it had colorful spring flowers in the background. I had a feeling I was going to need some cheer for this. "Fill me in."

I hadn't started my career with any desire to be an expert witness. And certainly not one who was nationally registered and got calls from all over the country. That hadn't been my goal. But our purposes in life aren't always clear to us, are they?

"I've got a guy who killed his wife."

Dead wife, I jotted.

"The weird part is, I need you to interview his wife."

Reading what I'd just written, I said, "I'm not real successful with dead people." I'm also not callous, but Sheila seemed to bring out the dark in me.

Or maybe it was the stuff we dealt with that did it.

"This is a different wife." Sheila replied, her serious and detached tone unchanged. "James Todd was a bigamist. Twice, actually. I spoke with Jane Hamilton, his first wife, early this morning. Seems to be in some kind of denial. I may need you to meet with her, too."

"He was married to three women?" What a guy.

"Yeah."

"Doesn't that make him a polygamist?" Like it mattered. I was just trying to take it all in. *Bigamy, deceit,* I wrote.

"No, just twice a bigamist. He married Lee Anne Todd, the murder victim, while he was married to Jane. Kept them both for a couple of years and then divorced Jane, apparently without either of the women being the wiser."

"What was he doing, a test run, to see which woman he preferred?"

"Who knows?" Sheila's disgust was obvious. "But he wasn't satisfied with wife number two, either. He married wife number three, Marla Anderson, last year, while still married to Lee Anne. Several months ago he asked Lee Anne for a divorce. She refused. She'd been spying on him, following him. She found out about wife number three, including the fact that Marla is an heiress, and threatened to expose him unless he paid her to be quiet. We think that's why he killed her."

"For what? To avoid a bigamy charge? I mean, what was he looking at? A fine?"

"Technically he could have done a little jail time, but avoiding the bigamy charge wasn't his motive. Money was. If Lee Anne exposed him, his marriage to Marla would be legally void. Marla would know that their relationship was a hoax, and all that money would no longer be his. He either had to resign himself to paying Lee Anne forever to buy her silence—and to living with the threat of exposure hanging over him—or he had to get rid of her."

"Do you know this or is it just theory at this point?" I knew how Sheila generally operated. Theory to proof, rather than proof to theory like some of the other prosecutors I'd worked with. Either way was fine with me. I just liked to know, going in, if I was up against opinion or fact.

"A bit of both. We've got some substantial evidence, but a lot of it is going to rely on the character witnesses. I need you to talk to Marla. Let me know if you think she's telling the truth about this guy. She insists he's the gentlest man she's ever met. Never shown any temper or violence. If you think she's lying I might need you to testify."

"Okay." I was interested. Very interested.

"She's hostile at this point."

I wasn't surprised. The woman was married to a liar. Was probably in love with a liar. And, for now, she was desperate to believe a liar.

"I'm assuming spousal privilege doesn't come into play?"

"Right. At the moment, anyway. Their marriage is void, but now that he's a widower, they can always remarry. He's out on bond."

So he might still get the money anyway. If Marla Anderson believed in him long enough to marry him again. I liked it better when life was fair.

"You said you already spoke with his first wife?" I read my notes. "Jane Hamilton."

"Yeah."

"Does she remember him being violent?"

"She says he wasn't, but I've got some suspicious domestic violence police reports...."

"Suspicious how?"

"The cops were called, but not by her."

"Who called them?"

"The hospital."

"Jane Hamilton was accident-prone?" I guessed. I'd seen it before. More than once.

"Apparently. Or her husband was and she just happened to be in the way each time."

"Did the police investigate?"

"Yeah. They were concerned, but there was never enough evidence to file charges."

"Why are you so sure he killed Lee Anne?"

"He was the last person known to be with her. His

fingerprints were found in her car. Footprints found at the edge of the cliff match his shoe size. There was bruising on her back that wasn't explained by the fall. And the way she landed, the distance out from the edge of the cliff points to her having been pushed hard rather than falling. He had motive...."

"Who's paying for his defense?" I asked, though I'd have bet that I already knew the answer.

"Wife number three."

I'd have won my bet.

CHAPTER ONE

"JANE, TALK TO ME."

Jane's heart pounded as Brad's gaze met hers. Pressure, rising like a tidal wave from within, strangled her throat and throbbed behind her eyes.

She had enough to handle without Brad Manchester adding to the mix.

Sitting on a log in the wilderness in Illinois, part of a two-hundred-acre plot of land Brad had purchased with plans to someday build a cabin on it, Jane just wanted a couple of hours away from all the stress. The basket and water bottles, remains of their picnic lunch, still lay on the blanket spread a few feet away. Brad sat with them.

They'd left their homes in Allenville, a suburb of Chicago, only hours ago. Right now it felt like days.

The rough bark dug into the backs of her thighs through her jeans. A twig poked just behind her right ear. Strands of chocolate-brown hair hung loose from the clip holding her twisted bun. She'd sweated off most of her makeup—she never left home without it on—an hour into the day-long hike.

Her employees would look askance if they could see her now. As the editor of a new national women's magazine, with only initial backing and the threat that if they failed they'd be left in the dust, Jane prided herself on being always professional and well put together.

She didn't usually let her hair down.

Except when she was with Brad. He was her buddy. Safe.

Usually.

"You've been distracted all day," Brad said now.

Jane nodded, not quite meeting his eyes.

"We've been friends what, two years?"

"About that." Long enough to see the countless women who flitted in and out of his life almost as frequently as he changed his underwear. And to share in many, many court triumphs with him as he represented abused women seeking freedom.

"I've seen you happy, worried, angry and exhausted, but I've never seen you look so…lost."

She felt lost. And utterly alone.

"Obviously something serious has happened. What I can't figure out is why you aren't talking to me about it."

At her silence, his expression intensified.

"I thought we could tell each other anything."

Not quite. But almost.

"Have I done something to…"

"No! Oh, God, no, Brad. You… I… You're my best friend."

"You sure about that?"

"Yes."

"Okay, then, why don't you tell Uncle Brad what's got you so distracted that you completely missed my last three attempts at conversation?" His words, while cloaked in levity, increased the tension tightening her chest.

Funny how one phone call could undo years' worth of moving on.

"I'm sorry," she said, trying to recall anything he'd been talking about during the lunch stop.

"Don't be sorry. Just tell me what's wrong." He sat forward, feet on the ground, his arms resting on his knees.

"Did your doctor say something? Are you sick?"

He knew she'd been for her yearly physical a few weeks before.

"No." She shook her head. "I'm in perfect health." Physically, at least. And she was determined to be so mentally and emotionally, too. She'd fought too hard to let someone else win now.

"You got another threat, then," he guessed. It was a testament to how rattled she was by the call she'd received that morning that she hadn't thought once about the threats. She'd received a couple of pieces of anonymous mail at work, one each for the past two weeks.

Do what's right or else.

Until this morning, the threats had occupied her thoughts almost constantly. She'd read the words countless times, trying to figure out what they meant. What they referred to.

And hated that she came up blank.

"No," she said. "Though I got a call from the police yesterday. They found no fingerprints other than mine and Marge's on the letters. The envelopes had been handled by so many people they couldn't identify anything. They've talked to everyone and didn't find anything." Which hadn't been a surprise to her. She knew her staff. If any of them had a problem with her, they'd talk to her face-to-face.

"So what happens now?"

"They're running a search for similar crimes on other magazines, particularly those dealing with women's issues. They're also checking into relatives, spouses and ex-spouses of the women at Durango."

Jane wasn't all that upset by a check on the women's shelter where she and Brad both volunteered. Extra police protection wasn't a bad thing when you were afraid for your life.

"What about you? Do they think it's safe to continue going into the office?"

"I can't not work."

"That's not what I asked."

"They're running extra patrols around the office, and around my house, too. And they suggested I hire someone...."

"And did you?"

"Marge made some calls. Found a guy who's going to be starting on Monday at *Twenty-Something*."

"What about at home?"

"In the first place, I can't afford a round-the-clock private bodyguard," Jane said. "In the second place, the danger is clearly at the office—even the police think so. I haven't received any threats at home. And in the third place, I couldn't stand to have someone shadowing my every move. I'd rather take my chances."

Brad didn't look entirely convinced. "So why couldn't you tell me about this?"

"I just forgot...." As soon as the words slipped out, Jane wished she could take them back. Brad would've been satisfied with the threats as the reason for her unusual mental absenteeism.

Brad stood up. "Forgot?" He shook his head. "What's going on, Jane?"

As Jane thought about the phone call from the Ohio prosecutor, she tried to figure out what she could tell Brad. Brad Manchester might be determined to live footloose and fancy-free, but he was also one of the most decent men she'd ever known. He truly cared.

And while he dated a lot of women, maybe because there were so many of them, Jane was the one he turned to when he needed a friend.

He wanted to return the favor.

She didn't blame him. She didn't blame anyone.

Maybe that was the problem. Maybe she should blame her creep of an ex-husband. Or the woman who'd stolen him away from her.

Except... Lee Anne was... And James was... Jane did blame herself.

When she could stand the internal cacophony no longer, Jane jumped up, stepping over the backpack she'd worn on the hike. She stopped a couple of feet from the ledge directly in front of them. It wasn't a sharp drop, but it was the high point of the property. It seemed as though they were in heaven up here. At the top of the world. And for as far as she could see there was nothing but green, trees, hills, brush, grass and wildflowers. Wilderness.

No pavement. No cars. No people.

No subterfuge.

Sometimes, looking into Brad's deep brown eyes was a lot like standing there at the top of the world. They'd managed to rise above life's complications to form a bond that was near perfect.

He was the truest friend she'd ever had.

"I've never trusted anyone like I trust you," she blurted.

Her career she had down pat. But not this.

Not being emotionally vulnerable. Or out of control.

Jane continued to survey the world. "I... This is just something I have to handle on my own."

"You sure about that?"

Hell, no. She wasn't sure about much of anything at the moment. Except that shc had to be strong, had to take care of herself.

"This is me you're talking to, Jane. I'm on your side, remember?"

There really was no reason to panic. She'd had a phone call. A blast from the past. Nothing that affected the woman she'd become. Nothing that affected her life today.

And the threats—she'd hired protection for herself and her staff. The police were working diligently on that investigation.

"Maybe I can help." Brad was just a few feet away.

Her only close friend. A lawyer. The best.

"I got a call this morning." The statement could have been random.

"Who from?" He'd come closer.

"A prosecutor. In Ohio. Chandler, Ohio."

"That's where your ex moved after your divorce, isn't it?"

"Right." It didn't surprise her that he'd remembered a detail he'd heard only once—one night when they'd shared a bottle of wine and exchanged divorce horror stories. "James has been charged with murder. They want me to testify."

Two short sentences. Manageable.

"What!" Brad turned her around, brought her back toward their blanket. His hands were surprisingly gentle on her shoulders. Odd that she'd even noticed. He'd touched her before. A hand on her back as she preceded him into the theater. Or a restaurant. And she'd never reacted. Brad meant nothing to her in the physical sense, no matter how attractive other women found him.

"Who'd he kill?" His fingers slid from her shoulders, but the warmth of his touch lingered. "And why would they think you know anything about it?"

Another surge of panic swept over her.

Jane wasn't a complete stranger to court. She volunteered at Durango, a Chicago women's shelter, helping battered women with professional writing like letters and résumés, and helping them gain healing through personal writing, too. She'd been asked to be a supportive shoulder during domestic abuse trials several times. That was how she'd met Brad. He offered free legal advice at the same shelter.

Jane also volunteered as a receptionist one night a week for a local Victim Witness program, a government-funded project that provided free support to victims obtaining protection orders.

She was seasoned. The call that morning, while disturbing, shouldn't be debilitating her.

"They say he killed Lee Anne." She couldn't understand it. Couldn't seem to focus on anything but the words. They just repeated themselves, again and again, in her mind.

"My God. Lee Anne's dead?"

Brad sounded as though he'd known the woman, rather than just having heard about James's second wife from Jane. She nodded.

"What happened?"

"She was found at the bottom of a cliff." Jane shuddered, glancing back at the expanse below them. Standing atop the cliff—looking out—could seem like heaven and could quickly become hell. "Her hyoid bone was broken, which could point to strangulation, but there was no obvious bruising there. But there was some on her back." Jane rattled off the facts as though reading a finance report. They seemed just as distant, just as impersonal. "Lee Anne apparently told a friend that she was going to meet James for lunch. But they never made it to the restaurant she'd said they were going to. Her car was found at the base of a trail leading up to the cliff. James's truck was spotted in the same area and there were footprints his size at the cliff. Broken foliage and dirt patterns indicated a struggle. His fingerprints were found inside her car and when questioned, he'd said he was at home that morning, alone. They told him his truck had been seen near the cliff. After which he admitted to being in the woods with her, to being in her car, but he claims that they talked and that she was still sitting in her car, perfectly fine, when he left."

"How long ago was this?"

"Six weeks."

"They've had enough time to go over the body, then. Did they find anything to indicate that she'd been pushed?"

"The prosecutor, a Sheila Grant, said that the coroner found fingerprint-shaped bruising beneath the skin on her back."

Brad practiced family law these days, mostly representing abused women, but he'd also done a stint as a prosecutor, so he was familiar with the challenges Sheila Grant could be facing. From everything Jane had heard, he'd been a great prosecutor. And he'd been stifled by politics and people above him who were apt to seek convictions and sentences based on factors other than the severity of the crime. Especially if there was an election or a point to prove.

A breeze blew through, rustling leaves and cooling clothes still damp from the sweat she'd worked up on their hike. Chilling her skin.

"What exactly does Ms. Grant want from you?"

And that's where her throat froze up.

"Jane?"

"She wants me as a character reference."

Brad studied her from below his lowered eyebrows and she could almost hear that talented brain of his whizzing along. A prosecutor would only seek character testimony from someone who had information that would support the murder theory.

"Did you tell her you would testify?"

"Yes." And then she quickly added, "But I don't know what good I'm going to be. It's not like I expected something like this. I'm in total shock. The James I thought I knew was weak and selfish, but he wasn't a murderer."

"Very few people have any idea someone they loved is capable of murder," Brad said, taking her hand in another unusual show of physical support. Something she rarely needed.

She let him link her fingers with his and held on.

"I come up against it again and again," he was saying. "The shock. The disbelief. You know this as well as I do. With all of the articles *Twenty-Something* has done, your volunteer work and the editorials you've written, you're as much an expert on domestic abuse as I am. I'm sure you can quote statistics."

Probably. Being the CEO of a start-up magazine focusing on issues facing today's young women did have its benefits. And what she hadn't gleaned from her work on *Twenty-Something,* she'd learned through her years of volunteering.

Domestic abuse. Brad's words, couched in generalities, lay between them. She'd told Brad her ex-husband had been unfaithful. His infidelity had been the reason for their divorce.

She'd told him the truth. At least, as much of it as she'd known.

"Sheila Grant told me this morning that James is a bigamist. And that I'm one of his victims."

A victim. Jane hated the sound of that. The feel of it. As though she'd been branded.

Brad leaned back, staring at her. "You're still married?"

"No!" Shaking her head, she squeezed his hand. And still didn't let go. She'd been hanging out with Brad for a couple of years now and this was the first time they'd held hands. "My divorce is perfectly legal," she said. "But it hadn't happened yet when he married Lee Anne. He wasn't just having an affair with her—he'd taken her to Vegas and married her."

"Then, he wasn't really married to her at all."

"Apparently he'd asked her for a church wedding, complete with an Ohio marriage license, after our divorce, still without telling her about his first marriage. It was for their anniversary. He told her the Vegas wedding didn't feel legitimate enough."

"What a guy."

"Yeah and it gets worse. He married a third time, about eighteen months ago."

"Let me guess, he didn't bother divorcing Lee Anne first."

"Right."

Brad frowned, taking on the look she'd seen him wear in the courtroom. His thinking face. "If he doesn't want her around anymore, why not just divorce her?"

Jane relayed what Sheila Grant had told her about the triangle in Chandler, Ohio. Some supposition. Some not.

Brad seemed to agree with the prosecutor's blackmail theories, but Jane didn't know what to think. The whole thing—James being a bigamist, her not knowing that her husband was lying to her in such a fundamental way—was just too unbelievable.

A lot of men could pull off an illicit relationship on the side. But a second marriage? And she hadn't even suspected?

Where was the strong, capable woman who'd been given the chance to head up a new national magazine? Who stood at the head of a Chicago boardroom and justified spending thousands of dollars on copy and cover art, layout and gloss? Who, in her spare time, helped vulnerable women find their feet?

Could the real Jane Hamilton please stand up? A mental version of the old television show *To Tell the Truth* played in her brain. Or should that be, Could the real Mrs. James Todd please stand up?

She was spiraling out of control. Didn't know herself. Didn't know what

"Did he hit you, Jane?"

Brad's softly spoken question broke through her internal torment.

"No! Of course not." She'd have known what to do about that.

They stood there, peering into each other's eyes. She tried to smile at the man who'd become such an important part of her life.

"But he hurt you."

Of course he had. He'd been unfaithful to her. He'd been her mentor. Her professor. And then her friend and lover and husband. She'd looked up to him. Learned so much from him. And...

Was she really so pathetic that she'd overlooked

enough lies that he'd been able to hide a second family? Had she been that desperate to keep James in her life?

Brad was watching her and the idea of him seeing her as a helpless victim felt far too threatening.

For no reason. Her sense of self-worth came from within.

Still she broke away and dropped down to the blanket. She held the container with the fruit they hadn't yet eaten, but didn't open it.

"I wasn't abused." The constriction in Jane's throat lessened. "There were a couple of accidents that were blown out of proportion. That's all. Sheila Grant got hold of some old police reports."

Brad sat down beside her, his long frame seeming to take up far more of the blanket than it had earlier.

"You called the police?"

She shook her head. "I told you, they were accidents. Which the doctor in the emergency room felt compelled to report. The police asked some questions, and they left. No charges were filed." Holding the container of fresh strawberries in her lap, she glanced up at him. "God knows, I appreciate the law that requires medical personnel to notify police whenever they see something that suggests abuse, but in my case, those calls just caused a lot of embarrassment. James was a professor at the local university. Well liked. Respected. He was not a wife beater."

Brad's expression remained completely focused. "Do you have any idea why Ms. Grant would be interested in the reports?"

"Apparently they were filed with suspicion."

"Meaning that while no one was charged, the investigating officer wasn't convinced a crime hadn't been committed."

Right. So Sheila Grant had explained, though that morning had been the first Jane had heard of any suspicion.

"What happened? Tell me about the accidents."

"I fell down the stairs once and before you say anything, yes, I'm positive I tripped. James did not push me, though the doctor, and the cop, too, for that matter, kept trying to get me to say he did."

"So James was there."

"Yes, we were going downstairs together. And no, we weren't fighting."

His head slightly lowered, Brad watched her with a sideways glance. "And you're sure there's no way he pushed you."

"It would have been physically impossible. I was behind him. As a matter of fact, he helped break my fall."

"And the other time?"

"We were playing tennis. We had one of those machines that shot balls over the net to us. He was demonstrating. I ran into his swing and caught his arm with my nose."

"How were things between you then?"

"He was wonderful, picked me up and ran me to the car, not caring that I was dripping blood on his new upholstery. He rushed me to the hospital and was everything any wife could want in a loving husband."

"I meant before the incident. How were things between you on the tennis court?"

Oh. Jane thought back, her chest getting tight again. And then she reined herself in.

"I think we were fighting," she said slowly. "Or had been. It's hard to remember. There were so many times we were at odds there toward the end."

"And he never lifted a hand to you?"

"Not once. Ever. He never backed me into a corner, or even touched me in anger."

Brad moved and Jane jumped. Reaching toward her, he tucked a wayward strand of hair back behind her ear. "If the suspicions are false, why was it so hard for you to tell me about it?"

"Do you have any idea how humiliating it is to know that I considered myself in love with a man who was so not in love with me that he was actually married to someone else at the very same time he was married to me?"

Brad frowned and she continued, "After Sheila Grant first called this morning, I started thinking about my marriage. Looking for signs James might have given of what he was doing, clues that I missed. Something to restore my faith in my judgment. And it took me right back to square one. Before, I thought I'd only missed the signs of him being unfaithful—having a girlfriend. That kind of thing happens all the time. But *bigamy?* I missed the fact that James was someone else's husband at the same time that he was mine. Why didn't I see it before? And how do I know I wouldn't miss something that big in the future? How could I ever trust myself to know? The phone call also confirms that I wasn't such a great wife. Not only did my husband seek sex elsewhere, he sought a wife elsewhere, too."

How much of that had been Jane's fault? James had obviously loved her at some point—he'd wanted to marry her. What had she done to cause him to lose interest?

"By all accounts that man is sick, Jane. His choices are no more a reflection on you than they are on the other two women he lied to."

"Which doesn't negate the fact that I didn't see what he was doing. Didn't even suspect. I was an easy target."

"You were a young woman, a student, who trusted her mentor. And later her husband."

"I trusted an untrustworthy man." Jane hated being unsure of herself. It reminded her too much of her life with James.

Her life before *Twenty-Something*.

"The way Emily trusted me."

Emily. Brad's ex-wife and his biggest scar.

"That woman adored me," he continued. "And you know I say that with shame, not ego. I loved her, but not any more deeply than I'd loved other people."

He'd told her all about his guilt over drinks after their first time in court together with a Durango resident.

"I cared enough about Emily that I stayed, even after it became obvious to me that our relationship had run its course. I kept trying to be as happy in our marriage as she needed me to be. As happy with her as she was with me during those times when she believed I loved her. She stayed because she kept hoping that, with time, our relationship would grow and we'd find the closeness she craved. I hung on for several years trying to fall in love with her as much as she loved me. A lot of people were hurt over my inability to give up. I robbed her of several years of happiness, of the chance to find someone who could love her more deeply than I could. And still Emily hung on, waiting. Believing in me, in the vows we took. Does that make her somehow less?"

"No." Jane got his point. But she wasn't Emily. "There's a major difference here, Brad."

"What's that?"

"She was married to a good and decent man who was trying to love her the way she needed him to."

"And you thought you were, too."

"Right, but the guy I was married to was apparently a two-bit schmuck."

"His problem. Not yours. It sounds to me like you were a faithful wife, committed to the marriage. Nothing more." With his arms resting on his bent knees, Brad glanced straight at her again. "Unless there's more. Sheila Grant seems to think so…"

"Why are you trying so hard to paint me abused?" He hadn't actually said as much, but she knew what he was implying. She could tell he didn't believe her. Indignation was good for the soul. Or at least for distracting her from her own weakness.

"I'm not sure," he said, as frank with her as ever. "Maybe because I've seen that frightened look a hundred times before but never in your eyes."

The compassion in his voice brought her close to tears. "Why are you doing this?"

"Doing what? Being a friend?"

"Climbing inside my head."

"I don't know," he said again. After a moment of silence, he added, "You're struggling. And I care."

She needed him to care and was glad he did. But he was pushing. And they didn't pressure each other. It was part of what made their unique friendship so successful.

"It occurs to me for the first time—" Brad paused, and Jane braced herself "—that things about you fit the profile of an abused woman."

They did not. He was just wrong about that. If she fit the profile, he'd have seen that before today. "Like what?"

"Like the fact that in the two years I've known you, you haven't been on a single date."

"Come on, Manchester. It's a new world out there. One where a woman doesn't need to have a man to be complete."

"No, but she doesn't generally need to avoid them, either."

"I've been busy getting a magazine off the ground, in case you haven't noticed."

"You stay busy, and yet you're the most isolated person I know. You have a lot of acquaintances, a lot of people who look up to you and care for you, but none, that I know of, other than me, with whom you're really close. You help them, but who helps you?"

"I've always been a bit of a loner. And a nurturer. I know what I want and that's okay." She knew herself. Liked herself. Was overall happy with who she was and where she was in her life. "There's nothing wrong with being different as long as you're happy that way. Look at my mom."

Jane's parents hadn't been married. Brad not only knew the story, he'd met her mother once.

Her dad, a professional military man, had traveled constantly, moved all over the world, and her mother, a small-town girl, hadn't been able to sign on for that kind of life. They'd continued to love each other, to see each other occasionally, until he'd been killed in the Gulf War when Jane was twelve.

Later, her mom married a local man, a single father with one son a few years younger than Jane. Her husband had eventually retired from the manufacturing firm where he'd worked all his life and taken her to Alaska to live with him on a fishing boat. Jane heard from them a few times a year, when they were in port.

The important thing was, they were happy. They'd all been happy.

"Besides, you're one to talk. I don't see any real relationships in your life, either. And I'm not calling you abused."

"I hurt a sweet woman very badly," Brad reminded her. "I can't even think about getting serious with anyone unless I'm positive that I can give her my whole heart."

Jane stared at him. "So you do want to marry again someday?" She'd been worried about him. Worried he was going to waste his life on one-night stands. Which would have been fine if it made him happy, but it didn't seem to. He tried too hard to stay busy—as though he was outrunning his dissatisfaction.

Brad's mother had been killed in a car accident when he'd still been too young to remember her. And his father had passed away four years before, from a massive heart attack.

Aside from a few distant cousins, he was alone in the world.

"I want a family, sure," he said. "But not unless I meet someone I know I can love forever."

So maybe his constant dating was more than she'd realized. Maybe he was searching...

"Do you think that really happens?" Jane asked, curious—and also relieved to be talking about something besides her.

"I like to believe it can," he said and then sent her a grin. "I'm certainly doing extensive research on the topic."

That was more like the Brad she knew. "Well, spare me the details, but do tell if you find a definitive answer."

And then, just like that, his face grew serious once again. "I'm more interested in finding answers for you, right now," he said. "I'm concerned about you, Jane."

"And I'm telling you there's no reason to be. The phone call shocked me today. I need some time to get used to the idea of having been a bigamist's wife. But I'm fine. Really."

"Okay, but I want you to think about something for me."

"What's that?"

"Durango's number one profile characteristic of an abused woman."

The list was posted in the main gathering room at the shelter. Jane knew it by heart.

And at the top:

She lives in denial.

Damn him

CHAPTER TWO

BRAD WASN'T SURE why he was pushing so hard. The whole reason he and Jane were good together, the one thing that had allowed their unusual friendship to work, was the lack of expectation for more than either wanted to give.

They cared about each other, they were open to soul-deep confidences, to emotional intimacy, but they didn't require it of each other. And they never got personal, physically.

Other than that time she'd had the flu and he'd taken care of her.

And the lump. Brad had been in the shower and found a lump in his prostate. He'd called Jane first, his doctor second. And a day later she'd treated him to drinks at their favorite neighborhood pub to toast his perfectly normal good health.

As he recalled, she'd laughingly left him to it that night when he'd spotted a red-haired beauty sitting alone at the bar....

With so much unsaid between them, they sat on their picnic blanket silently staring out over a land that didn't really hint at all the danger that lurked in the world. Not that Brad spent a lot of time pondering life's dangers. He knew the dangers would find them without their help.

What they needed to figure out was how to be happy regardless of the dangers.

Jane was eating a strawberry; juice dripped off her lower lip. Funny, he'd never noticed how full her lips were...

Maybe he should stick to figuring out how, on Monday, he was going to fight a client's husband for the support she deserved after having put up with his emotional abuse for more than twenty years.

"You're wrong, you know?"

"About what?"

"About me being abused."

Brad met Jane's gaze and saw that she meant it. So why didn't he believe her?

"After the tennis incident...I wasn't sure. The doctor made such a big deal of the direction of the blow. He said that James would've had to pull his elbow back into my nose to have broken it the way he did, not going forward for a shot as he claimed."

"How did it seem to you?"

Jane's pause unsettled him. He dealt with similar silences too often. With intelligent, strong women who'd been so emotionally broken down that they second-guessed themselves in spite of their abilities.

"I honestly couldn't say." He wished her words surprised him. "One minute I was standing there, the next minute I was on the ground in the most excruciating pain I'd ever known. My head was pounding so hard I couldn't hear. Couldn't see."

"Did you tell the police you didn't know what happened?"

"Not at the time. I was too out of it. I just went with what James told me had happened. But a few days later, after James and I went back to work, I kept thinking about how angry he'd been, and what the doctor had said. The doubts set in. James left for a graduate study trip and while he was gone I went to the Victim Witness office in town, just in case I was reading things wrong. Since their sole purpose is victim support, I figured they'd know if I needed help. I told them everything. They said that there was no evidence of abuse."

"Even with what the police and doctor had said? Even with your doubts?"

"They said that my doubts were indicative of a problem in my marriage, but that as far as obtaining a protection order was concerned, I didn't have enough evidence."

Jane was fiddling with the lid of the strawberry container. Opening and closing it. Watching the movement. Not at all the head-up-and-shoulders-straight woman he knew.

"Maybe they were wrong."

"I don't think so, Brad. I think my doubts were a result of professionals who had to do their jobs or risk potential lawsuits. While I was at Victim Witness another woman came in. She was bruised and swollen and she'd been sitting in the outer office, waiting for the counselor to be done with me. She could hardly speak. She was crying, but one eye was so swollen the tears couldn't escape.

"She had two little kids with her, younger than four. They huddled against her and even as scared as she was, she protected them fiercely.

"Seeing them was a life-changing moment for me. That was what abuse looked like. I couldn't get that family out of my mind and from then on I quit feeling sorry for myself. I made the decision that I was going to spend my life helping women not to live like that. I started volunteering as a receptionist at that office the very next week."

Jane had never told him how she got her start with the women they helped. He'd never asked, assuming that she'd somehow fallen into it through her work—as he had.

"James and I had some bad fights after that," she added, her voice soft and distant. "And not once did I get hurt. Nor was I ever physically afraid of him. Like I said. The incidents were accidents."

Brad didn't believe her. But he didn't have any real reason not to, so kept his thoughts to himself. Maybe he'd seen too much of the other side. Maybe knowing that, statistically, one in two women suffered some form of spousal abuse had clouded his judgment. Maybe his perspective was too jaded.

And maybe not.

"Besides, one thing I know is that I'm more than capable of taking care of myself and those around me."

Jane's description fit the woman he knew.

"I've always had preservation instincts," she continued, her voice going stronger. And when she smiled, Brad smiled with her. "I remember when I was a kid and I couldn't wait for my dad's visits. He'd only be with us a few days or weeks at a time, and those were the highlight of the year. For both my mom and me. Except for one thing."

"What's that?"

"He used to tickle me to the point that it hurt. I hated that. And the more I struggled, the more he tickled. It was a game to him but it wasn't one I enjoyed playing. But I wasn't strong enough to get away."

Brad didn't like the game at all. The older man had been way out of line, holding his own daughter captive.

"It didn't take me long to figure out how to save myself, though," Jane continued, not sounding the least bit put out or scarred by the incidents.

"How?"

"I'd scream at a really high pitch. My mom couldn't stand the noise and would tell my dad to stop in that voice that meant he'd better do it now."

"And did he?"

"Of course. Every time."

And so she'd solved her problem. A little girl figuring a way to get the best of a grown man. That was his Jane—if one way didn't work, she'd find another. Maybe he'd been worrying about nothing. Though that wasn't like him.

They were silent for a long time, each lost in his and her own thoughts. It was a comfortable silence, one they shared a lot when they were together like this. And then Jane said, "I am afraid of something, though." The tentative tone in her voice got his full attention.

"What's that?"

"The picture you painted of me—alone—I didn't realize it was so obvious."

"That you keep yourself detached from all of us?" Not from him—except physically.

"I..." Jane's eyes revealed uncharacteristic hesitancy when she raised her head and met his gaze. "Can I tell you something?"

"You know you can."

"It's personal and embarrassing and..."

"Then this is probably the day for it."

She hesitated a moment longer and then said, "What James did—the mental cruelty, the infidelity—it killed my ability to...you know...want...things."

She couldn't be saying what he thought she was

saying. Not Jane. She was femininity personified. Gorgeous. A head turner. And…

"Are you saying you don't want…*things?*"

They were up on a private wooded hill, away from the rules of life. The rules of Brad and Jane. What they said here would be forgotten once they descended to real life.

And he'd all but bullied her to confide in him.

She shook her head. "I haven't had so much as a tingle…down there…since my divorce."

Brad was shocked. He knew she hadn't dated, but…

Thinking of Jane sexually was taboo. So he hadn't. But in the back of his mind, he'd assumed she…something. He'd never thought beyond that.

And didn't have any solid thoughts now, either. Their hill had turned into quicksand. An electrified quicksand for him.

"Have you talked to anyone about it? Professionally?"

"Yeah. But it didn't do any good. It just happens that way sometimes. More often with women, I'm told."

"It's probably just because you haven't been on a date in so long," he blurted, thinking of all the women he'd been with since he'd met her.

Brad liked sex. A lot. And he made no apology for that. The idea of being unable to experience those sensations…

"It's not like I don't get invitations," Jane said dryly. "I don't date because I'm not the least bit interested in the men who ask me out."

"You should meet more men, different men." His mind tried to fight its way out of the thickness encasing him. "I've got a couple of friends from law school. I could…"

He shouldn't have been relieved when Jane shook her head, preventing him from having to finish the offer. But he was.

"I know fine men, Brad. Successful, fun, funny men. Smart, introspective men. Older men. Younger men. Good-looking. Great-looking. Okay-looking…"

"And nothing?"

"Nothing."

"Maybe you're wired the other way," he suggested, hardly recognizing the tinny sound to his voice. Yeah, let her be gay. That would make him a hell of a lot more comfortable.

It would safeguard their friendship forever. Unless they both fell in love with the same woman.

"I'm not a lesbian." Funny how four words could weigh a man down and lift him up all at the same time. "I think, with as much time as I spend around women, I'd know if they pushed my buttons. They don't."

Brad's throat was too dry to speak. So he sat there, hands resting nonchalantly on his knees, wondering what the hell was the matter with him. He talked to a lot of women about sex—those he was having it with, and some he wasn't. He was completely comfortable with the topic.

"I was perfectly normal," Jane continued as though now that her demon had been unleashed, she felt better letting it all out. And he understood fully the old saying about being careful what you asked for.

He'd pushed her to open up to him, egotistically certain that he was the one who should be there for her in her time of need.

"And you…felt things." Some masochistic part of

his soul made him ask. He didn't want to picture Jane with another man. Didn't want to picture her naked. Or sexual in any way. She was Jane. His Jane. Asexual.

Which was exactly what she was telling him. The asexual part.

And that wasn't right. This beautiful, warm woman asexual?

"Oh, yeah. So much it made me his slave." Jane's eyes widened as she spoke, and Brad knew he would never forget the stricken expression that came over her face. "And when James betrayed me, when he kept telling me that his infidelity was my fault, I…"

She stopped and Brad waited, focusing on the slight breeze that had passed over their picnic site.

"I haven't been the least bit interested in sex since," she finally said. "He killed it, Brad. And it's kind of hard to have a truly intimate relationship without that."

"I'm sure it's not dead, sweetie," Brad said now, grasping for anything that would keep his head above the sand. "You know the drill better than most. After any kind of mistreatment, these things take time. And the right person. The feelings are in there."

"I don't think so." Jane's eyes were clouded again. "It's been five years since my divorce."

"Jane, don't do this to yourself. Relax. I'm sure you're fine."

"Am I?" Clearly skeptical, she looked him up and down. "Take you for example," she said. "You're gorgeous. What woman in her right mind wouldn't see you and at least entertain a thought…feel some kind of attraction…"

What did a guy say to that?

"We… I've… It's been two years. We're together all the time. And I've never once…"

Good thing Brad's ego could afford the hit. Good, too, that relief eased some of the unintentional sting from her words.

"Maybe I'm not your type. And as for other men, you just haven't been open to it," he told her. "You've blocked that part of yourself. When you're ready…it'll be there."

"I wish I believed that. But after all this time, I just don't."

She sounded so…insecure. So lacking in worth. As though she had nothing of value to offer. So unlike the woman who'd, over the past two years, become the first person he called when he had news. The first person he thought of when the electricity went out, when he heard sirens and hoped no one was hurt, when he woke on Christmas morning.

Sex didn't define a person's value anyway. But Brad didn't say so. He knew it would be pointless. He knew from all the work he'd done with abused women that women had a tendency to intermingle personal worth with sexual attractiveness.

"You're wrong." His words were forceful. They needed to be. "Unless you don't do anything about it," he said, concerned for her. "If you shut yourself off, if you believe you'll never have those feelings again, you might not."

"I haven't shut myself off. I've…tried. With partners. And by myself. I even bought a toy off the Internet."

Jane's face turned red, but she didn't look away. She was sitting there, staring at him, completely open, and believing every word she said. Dictating her own life sentence.

Brad couldn't let that happen. Not to Jane. And he knew he could help her. Just like that.

"Then you haven't tried hard enough," he told her. He wasn't going to let her give up on herself.

"I have. I—"

"Listen." He cut her off. "I'm going to do something, and when I'm done, you'll know that you're all right. And then we're going to forget it ever happened. Okay?"

She watched him with her eyes wide. And while he stopped breathing, she nodded.

"We will never mention this…interlude. We will never repeat it."

She nodded again.

He could do this. No problem. He was the perfect choice because he wouldn't take advantage of her.

Brad was confident until he really looked at the woman sitting next to him. Her dark brown eyes. Perfect skin. Breasts that were so much more than they should be if he was going to not be attracted to them. Why had he never noticed them before?

His fingers brushed her face, her neck, slowly gliding over the softness.

"What are you doing?" Jane stared at him, but didn't pull back. If she had he would have stopped.

"I'm going to show you what you can feel." He was strangely unembarrassed by the hoarseness in his voice.

His body was hard and straining against his zipper. He knew how to ignore it.

"Are you game?"

"You're wasting your time." The near whisper sounded like a challenge to him.

"I don't think so."

"Brad?"

"Shh." He traced her lips with the pad of his thumb and they parted.

This wouldn't take long. The rational thought comforted him. One kiss should do it.

He leaned in, touched his lips to hers and lost himself to the burst of fire that shot clear down to his feet.

Brad had had enough women to appreciate when the sex was hot.

And yet when he felt Jane's lips against his he experienced a jolt so shocking, he felt like a first-timer.

Her eyes were still open, so he deepened the kiss, taking her lips fully with his. And when she didn't moan with need, he pushed a little further, opening her lips with his tongue.

She tasted of salt and strawberry. And something unknown, but very, very good. He played with her tongue. Teasing it. Exploring.

Alone.

She didn't resist, but she didn't join him, either.

Brad pulled away, not sure what he was going to do, and got a glimpse of Jane's face. Her eyes were almost closed, her features more relaxed than he'd ever seen them.

And yet not. Her mouth was slightly open. Waiting.

She might not be there yet, but she was getting there.

He kissed her again. And when her tongue still remained uninvolved, Brad moved his hand under the hem of her T-shirt, sliding his hand slowly up along the slender curve of her waist, lightly brushing the side of her breast. He thought she jerked a bit at his touch, but he couldn't be sure.

He couldn't stop, either. Not until he'd slid a finger

inside her bra. Touched her nipple, made it hard and...

It was already hard.

So they were done. He'd aroused her.

He kissed her once more, just to seal the deal with a response from her tongue.

It still didn't dance with him and he doubted himself. He knew a lot about women. He knew, for instance, that arousal wasn't the only reason nipples hardened.

And he knew that there was one sure way to tell if a woman was turned on. Brad reached for the button on Jane's jeans with only one thought in mind. Turn her on and get out.

He had to hand it to her. She was trying as hard as he was. She lifted her body, giving him easier access. And when it became obvious that it wasn't enough, she lifted her butt off the blanket and let him pull the pants down to her ankles. He took her panties, too, just for the sake of getting the task done quickly.

And when he started to salivate at the sight of her, he ignored the sensation. He had a job to do for his friend.

This wasn't about him or his needs. His body wasn't involved. Wasn't going to do anything. At least not now and never with Jane.

He was simply helping his friend.

At his urging, she spread her legs and his fingers went to work, knowing exactly what to do.

He found his mark on the first try. And discovered that she was already wet.

He could stop.

As soon as he made certain that Jane knew, without a doubt, what she was capable of feeling.

He didn't look at her face. Couldn't meet her eyes. He just focused on making her feel good.

And as soon as she'd climaxed, he'd get up and walk away. Let her put herself back together.

That's what he intended. That's what he told himself was going to happen.

It didn't.

CHAPTER THREE

MONDAY MORNING Jane was up, showered, had fed Petunia, her delicate and fragile rescue bird, and was on her way into the city from her Chicago suburb home before she was usually out of bed. She had a nine-thirty meeting with her art people and needed to stop at Durango on the way. She'd promised Josie Barker, one of the shelter's current residents, that she'd help her with her résumé that morning. Josie was applying for a job that could change her life.

And no matter how Jane managed to mess up her own life, she was going to make sure other women had a chance to improve theirs.

Josie was a lucky one. She'd gotten out of her abusive marriage early, before there were children. And before her self-esteem had been irreparably damaged.

"Jane?" Stopping on the steps up to Durango—a nondescript home close to Chicago's downtown with absolutely no signage or other giveaway characteristics to alert anyone to its true purpose—Jane glanced over her shoulder as she heard her name. Spinning, she recognized the woman coming up the street.

"Kim! What are you doing here?" And then, with a sick feeling in her stomach, she asked, "You aren't staying here again, are you?"

"No! Don't worry, I'm fine." The redheaded, freckle-faced woman stopped at the bottom of the three cement stairs, her hand on the black wrought-iron railing. "I was just coming to drop this off for Josie." She held up a hanger covered in dry-cleaning wrap. "For her interview. I'm early, actually, but Jason spent the night with my mom and I had way too much time on my hands this morning." Kim's cheer seemed forced, a state Jane knew well from her work with damaged women.

"I'm a little early, too," she said now, her own troubles fading. "Tell me how things are going."

"Good." Kim's red ponytail bobbed. "Really good. Brad's fantastic, just like you said he would be. I'll never be able to thank you enough for setting me up with him."

"Brad volunteers here regularly," Jane reminded her. "You'd have met up with him eventually if I hadn't called him."

Brad. She'd spent all of yesterday trying not to think about him. And all of last night, too.

"But who knows where I'd have been by the time he made his next visit." Kim shrugged self-consciously. "Anyway, I know he thinks he can't discuss my case with you, even though I told him he could, so I wanted you to know that I hired a second attorney, Christine Ryan, just to represent Jason."

"Why?"

The young woman's eyes filled with tears. "Because I'm too messed up where Shawn's concerned to know if I'm doing right by my son, or just knee-jerking. And I need Brad to be looking out for me."

Shawn. The husband. Whose actions had driven his wife to call the domestic abuse hotline and, with their young son, seek shelter at Durango.

"So he's still trying to get shared custody?"

"At the moment, I think he'd settle for visitation

rights. And I don't know, Jane. I mean, he never hurt Jason. He really loves him. And Jason misses him so much…"

"Shawn might not have hurt him physically, but I can assure you, Jason has suffered greatly from his father's aggressive actions."

Stay strong, Kim, Jane's inner voice urged. *Remember that what Shawn did was wrong. Against the law.*

She'd have said the words aloud, but Kim had already heard them many times. It was up to her whether or not she believed them and made choices accordingly. If Jane pushed, she was really no better than Shawn— browbeating Kim into doing what Jane thought was best.

At this stage, she could give Kim validation. Nothing more.

"Anyway," Kim said, shaking her head, "I'm glad I ran into you. My pastor came up to me at church yesterday and told me that Shawn had talked to him."

Jane's nerves stood on alert. "It's a violation of the protection order for him to use a third party to pass messages to you. Did you call the police?"

"No." Kim shook her head vehemently. "Shawn didn't know Pastor Rod was talking to me. I'm sure he'd rather he hadn't. Anyway, Rod said he'd really struggled with whether or not to say anything to me because of confidentiality issues, but said that he'd rather have betraying a confidence on his conscience than have someone hurt."

"So what did he say? Does he think that Shawn's a danger to Jason?"

"No. He thinks he's a danger to you."

Jane stepped back, the heel of her pump catching on the cement behind her. "Me?"

"Pastor Rod says that Shawn told him that this is all your fault. He says that if you hadn't called Brad right away, I'd have come home and given him a chance to apologize. He says he's lost his son because of you."

"He lost his son because he doesn't know how to be a man," Jane said, forcing her voice to communicate a calm she didn't feel. Could Shawn be behind the threats she'd been receiving at *Twenty-Something?* But what "right thing" could he want her to do?

It wasn't as if she had any power to influence custody orders.

Still, she'd let Detective Thomas know.

"Shawn's right, though, in one sense," Kim said, looking down and then back up. "I probably would have done just like he said and gone home and forgiven him."

Wishing she could take the young woman into her arms and make her world all better, Jane quietly asked, "And do you regret not doing that?"

"No!" The strength with which Kim's head shot up couldn't be ignored. "My gosh, Jane, I thank God every single night for you. If not for you, I'd have gone home again and again until he killed me. And maybe Jason, too."

"And now, if he comes within five hundred feet of you, he goes to jail," Jane said. "You keep your cell phone with you at all times, and you call the police if you so much as fear that he's close, right?"

"Right. I thank God for that phone and the protection order, too. Between those and you and Brad, I actually have hope of a life again. But I'm worried sick about you."

"Don't be," Jane assured her. "People like Shawn are cowards. They pick on those who they think won't hit back. And besides, we know how to keep ourselves safe and what to do if danger approaches. We don't have to live our lives in fear."

Jane had had all the self-defense classes right along with the victims at Durango. For cases just like this one. She might not be married to an abusive man, but she helped women who were.

Kim seemed bemused as she peered up at Jane. "You really aren't scared, are you?"

"No." Not of Shawn Maplewood at any rate.

"How do you do it?" Kim's voice was filled with longing. "How have you recovered so completely?"

"Recovered?" Jane asked, unsure what Kim was referring to.

"From your own abuse."

"What abuse?"

"Well…" Kim frowned. "I mean, I just…the girls and I assumed that since you were here, at Durango, you were, you know, a recovered victim.…"

"No, I'm not," Jane said, and then, something about the other woman's expression drove her to continue, to talk about the period in her life that she'd kept private for more than five years. Until Saturday.

"I thought I was once," she said. The admission was no easier the second time around and she wished she'd kept quiet two days before.

About so many things.

"I *was* married," she explained anyway. "My ex-husband used to be on me all the time, telling me what a disappointment I was, that kind of thing. I always seemed to be screwing up around him."

"Did you believe him?"

"Yes. Enough that I wanted to see a counselor. I wish now that I had." Jane smiled, but without humor.

No humor in her at all these days. She'd had sex

with Brad Manchester. She just couldn't believe it. And couldn't forgive herself, either.

She should have known better. She'd just screwed up a friendship that she really needed. But Kim didn't need to hear about that.

"Instead I just tried harder to make it work," Jane continued.

"You aren't married now," Kim said, her blue-eyed gaze serious. "What happened?"

"I caught James with another woman. I got out."

"Well, I'm glad you did. And that you're here," Kim said.

"Me, too." Jane smiled and reached for the hanger Kim had been switching from one hand to the other. "How about if I take that in for you?"

Kim gratefully released it. "Would you? Thanks. A double latte and a walk in the park before work just might be in order."

Wishing the young woman well, Jane turned to put her key in the lock.

"Jane?"

Kim's voice stopped her and she looked back.

"Yeah?"

"I owe you everything for saving my life. I'm worried about Shawn. Be careful. Okay?"

The tears that threatened prevented Jane from replying. She nodded instead.

"And for the record? I think that James guy should rot in hell for what he did to you."

CHAPTER FOUR

HE SHOULD HAVE CALLED JANE. On Sunday, Brad had taken an impromptu forty-mile bike ride instead. If the bike path had been expanded to its proposed seventy-mile length, he'd probably have gone the distance.

He could do that on a bike, no problem.

Going the distance in his personal life was another issue.

Brad had been around enough to know that some people just didn't have what it took to commit to a monogamous relationship. He wasn't convinced he was one of them, but it wasn't impossible.

He'd already broken one woman's heart. He was not about to risk doing it again.

And he didn't have sex with women except casually. For mutual recreational pleasure.

Now there was Jane.

It took Brad five minutes to drive from his home to the offices of Border, Manchester and Willow. Monday morning, while on that drive, Brad finally phoned his friend.

She didn't pick up.

He didn't blame her. They'd barely spoken on their hike down the hill on Saturday, other than to assure each other that what had happened would be forgotten. And he'd spent the two-hour trip back to town on the phone.

"Jane, hi, it's Brad." Great. He'd stopped identifying himself after a month of hanging out with her. "I was just calling to check on the time for Thursday's flight. Call me." He ad-libbed about as well as he'd greeted her.

He'd written down the time of her flight when he'd dropped her off Saturday evening. She was flying to Ohio to meet with Sheila Grant and he'd insisted on taking her to the airport.

He always took her to the airport. And picked her up, too.

Maybe by Thursday he would have forgotten Jane's long, sexy legs wrapped around his waist—her body grabbing hold of him, welcoming him inside.

Maybe.

If Thursday took a hundred years to get here.

JANE CALLED HIM BACK just as he was getting out of court. Brad's first instinct was to let the call go to voice mail. Communicating through technology devices was probably just what the doctor would order were they to go see someone about the mess they'd gotten themselves into.

He seemed to be all about stupid choices this week. "Hi," he said, sucking in the crisp spring air outside the courthouse.

"I was afraid you were avoiding me."

"Of course not."

"Don't."

"Don't what?"

"Lie to me. You've never lied to me. Don't start now."

There was a difference between lying and sparing someone's feelings. Like if one of his dates wore a dress he hated and he complimented the color. Or the fabric. Or maybe, in an extreme case, the way it matched... something.

"Okay, I've been avoiding you." This was Jane. They didn't hide or pull punches.

They didn't sleep together, either.

"Why?"

He'd reached his car, so he climbed in. He inserted the key in the ignition, but sat there without starting the engine. "That answer's obvious," he said, somewhat dryly.

"No, it's really not. Having sex was a mistake. We both said so, and agreed to forget it. It happened but now it's over. It would be a tragedy if we let fifteen minutes of insanity ruin a great friendship."

"So you're really okay with it?"

"I've had a moment or two, but overall, yeah, I'm okay with it."

"And with me?"

"I think so."

"I didn't mean it to happen, Jane. You have to know that. It was never my intention to have sex with you. At all."

"I know." He couldn't tell if her chuckle was sincere, or if she was just strong enough to fake it for the sake of their friendship.

"I would never take advantage of you. I just—"

"Brad, it's okay." She cut him off, still sounding like the Jane he'd always known. "I was there, too, you know. I could've said no."

Right. She could have. And she hadn't. He'd been so consumed with his own guilt that he'd lost sight of that part.

Damn. So did that mean she'd wanted to have sex with him? That she still wanted *him?*

Beginning to sweat, Brad turned the key so he could start the air-conditioning.

"I can't be best friends and have sex, too." He just put it right out there.

"I know. Me, neither."

"So where do we stand?" And why was he leaving it all up to her? What would he do if she said she wanted the sex more than the friendship?

"As best friends, I hope."

Okay. "I'm glad to hear that."

"So we're good?"

"Absolutely."

"No more avoiding me?"

"Nope." Just images of those long legs. He'd avoid those. But that he could handle.

"Whew." Jane sounded as relieved as he felt. "Thank heavens. I've spent the whole weekend feeling bereft, trying to imagine life without my buddy. It was awful. With everything going on in my life right now, the thought of losing you, too…"

"You aren't going to lose me," he promised. Though he wondered what she thought about the sex they'd shared. She had to have thought about it, too, over the weekend, but he didn't ask. Sex was something he and Jane were never going to discuss again.

They chatted for another ten minutes—almost as though proving that they could still hold a conversation. The case in Ohio was a safe topic. Jane was worried about the meeting there and truth be told, he was worried about it, too. About her.

When awkward silences fell, Brad hurried to fill

them. It would just take some time, he assured himself. They'd get back to who they'd been. He'd make certain of it.

He meant to tell Jane so as she was ringing off.

Instead, what came out was, "So...did it work?"

"Did what work?"

"Saturday." Since they were struggling to maintain a friendship that until now had been natural and easy, he wanted to know if the risk had been worth it.

"Don't ask, Brad. Don't ever, ever ask me about my sex life again. Don't even think about it. It's off-limits to you. And I promise not to talk to you about yours. Got it? That's the only way we can stay friends."

"Got it."

Brad hung up, relieved. He was glad to have the difficult conversation behind him, and satisfied that it had gone as well as could be expected. Better than expected. Great. Fantastic.

The best.

JANE WASN'T OUT of her art meeting five minutes before Marge Davenport, her senior editor, was at her office door with an envelope in her hand.

"We got another one," she said, her face pinched.

Jane stared at the envelope in Marge's hand, but didn't reach for it. "What does it say?"

"Same as the others. 'Do the right thing, or else.' That's it."

"Has Walt Overmeyer seen it?"

The private security guard had started that morning.

"Yeah, he's outside waiting to speak with you."

"Did you call Detective Thomas?"

"He's on his way over."

Jane cursed the fear that raced through her, making her weak.

"I WANT TO ASSURE YOU, Ms. Hamilton, we're taking this issue very seriously." The middle-aged detective stood with Jane just inside her closed office door, holding the newest threat letter in a ziplock bag.

Jane focused on the bisque-colored plaque hanging above the doorway. Bright flowers rimmed the ceramic piece, but they weren't why she'd purchased it or hung it there.

"The only thing we have to fear is fear itself." Franklin Delano Roosevelt, March 4, 1933.

"I've been in publishing long enough to know that you're never going to please everyone," she said now, glancing back at Detective Thomas. "You speak out against emotionally charged issues and there's always going to be someone having a bad enough day to need to have their grievances heard."

"So you've said."

"It's not like this is the first threat we've received."

"But it's the only one that's been repeated. Three times now."

Jane grew cold. "So what are you telling me? I can't stop living. I can't let some anonymous coward run me out of my world."

"I'm just saying that you need to proceed with extreme caution," Detective Thomas said. "If you've got vacation time, take it."

"I don't. And even if I did, where would I go? For how long?"

"I understand how difficult this is," the detective said. "Believe me, we're working as quickly as we can, trying to trace this. Unfortunately we're dealing with computer-generated messages on generic paper. We know from the postmark that whoever is sending these is mailing them from somewhere here in Chicago—probably from the same place each time. And based on the repetition, I'm guessing that this guy's serious."

"He might not be targeting me. They're addressed to the editor in chief."

"We are considering that he's angry with the magazine itself. But it would appear that he believes that you control whatever comes out of here. We have to assume that whatever it is he wants done is, in his opinion, under your control, as well."

Jane focused on the plaque.

"The guy's sending the letters here. What if this escalates and he targets the building?"

"We're posting extra people around the premises. A uniformed officer will be on guard at the security screening station at the main entrance. And screening officers are being assigned to the two private entrance doors, as well. They'll hand search everyone who tries to enter there."

The other tenants were going to love her.

She told Detective Thomas about her encounter with Kim Maplewood that morning and about Shawn's conversation with his pastor. He told her again to be careful.

"Don't go anywhere you don't absolutely have to go," he said. "Especially here in the city. And don't go anywhere alone."

"I've hired a private security company...."

"I've already met with Walt Overmeyer," the detective said. "He or one of his associates will also be walking you to and from your car and the building every day for the next little bit. I recommend that you hire them to watch your house at night, too. And in the meantime, we'll be doing all we can to get this guy."

Before he gets you, Jane finished silently, thanking the officer as she ushered him out.

She hadn't liked anything the man had to say.

He was there to help her. To protect her.

So why didn't she feel protected?

BRAD WAS BACK IN HIS OFFICE after an emotionally charged settlement conference when Jane called late Monday afternoon.

He answered the call on the first ring. He hadn't expected to hear from her again so soon.

"There's been another threat."

All thoughts of Saturday—and sex—flew out of his mind. "What does it say?"

"Same thing."

"So what in the hell does this guy want you to do?"

"He might be a woman, for all we know."

"Fine, what could this *person* possibly want you to do?"

"I have no idea." Jane's troubled sigh made it harder for him to stay detached. "Believe me, I'm driving myself crazy trying to figure it out," she continued. "I mean, how can I possibly do what this person wants if I don't know what it is?"

"What about nonthreatening letters to the editor?" Brad asked, hating this new feeling of helplessness he had where Jane was concerned. "Is there anything there that might tie in?"

"The police took everything we had and haven't found a connection. I've personally gone over every issue we've published in the past six months, tried to piece them together with a note or letter or phone call, but I can't come up with anything."

"But this person must think you know what he or she wants or why put on the pressure?"

"Detective Thomas suspects we're dealing with a narcissist. Or at least someone unhinged enough to overestimate their importance to me. The police are doing all they can, but how much time do I have before this person decides I'm not going to do what's right?"

"I guess that depends on what they want you to do."

"Right, and if I don't do it, what's the 'or else'?"

Brad had no answer to that, either, but whatever the "or else" meant, it couldn't be good.

"What about Durango? Did they find anything there?"

"Not yet, but I ran into Kim Maplewood this morning."

Brad straightened when he heard the name. His client was no longer officially associated with Jane, but she had a very angry ex-husband. "What'd she have to say?"

He was more uncomfortable than ever when he heard about Shawn's visit to his minister.

"He needs someone to blame in lieu of taking accountability for his own actions and since blaming Kim didn't work…" Brad let the thought trail off.

"I know. Thomas said he's going to bring Shawn in for questioning."

Brad was glad to hear it, but didn't feel any better about her safety. "And in the meantime?"

"I called Barbara Manley." Barbara was Jane's boss and the publisher of a much more established and highly respected national news magazine. Jane had written for

the publication before heading up *Twenty-Something*.
"The company is footing the bill for upgraded security
in our building and to have someone watch my house
at night, too."

"I'm glad to hear that. Keep your phone close by."

"I will."

"And your mace."

"I always do."

"Call me if you so much as hear the wind whistle."

"Okay."

"Or if you just plain get scared. I'm two minutes away
and sleep just fine on the couch."

He'd spent the night at her house before, when she'd
been sick. And a time or two on holidays when they'd
had more to drink than safe driving allowed.

"I'll be fine," she insisted and Brad had a feeling that
no matter how scared she might get in the middle of the
night, he was not going to be the one she called.

Whether Jane wanted to admit it or not, things had
changed between them.

The knowledge left him empty and sad. He was worried as hell about her. And helpless to do a damned thing
that would make the situation better.

THE BLACK SUIT? Or the red one? Black spoke of power
and authority. Its absence of color blocked emotional
accessibility. Black commanded respect. Red meant
energy. Strength. An ability to take action. It also spoke
of passion.

Jane threw the black suit into her suitcase. Black with
a white blouse. Elegant. Respectable.

And untouchable. She hoped.

She also hoped that the issue on clothing colors
that they'd run the previous year was more than just

psychological mumbo jumbo. She'd read every article before publication. Most of the stuff she'd heard before. Some she hadn't. Like the information about Elizabethan clothes colors.

Back then England had had Sumptuary Laws that dictated the colors people could wear. It had to do with immediate recognition of a social class, but also with the expense of fabrics and dyes. Red, black and white were colors worn mostly by royalty.

And the lower class...whatever. She really didn't care about Elizabethan clothes.

Adding her cosmetic bag, Jane zipped her suitcase shut and pulled it from bed to floor with ease. What she really cared about was that her flight to Ohio—to meet with the prosecutor in her ex-husband's trial—left in a little over three hours. Which meant Brad would be arriving momentarily.

She was nervous about the drive. About being alone with him. That last conversation on Monday, he'd sounded different by the time they hung up. A bit distant. And other than a quick call each evening to confirm that the unmarked security car was outside her house, Jane hadn't heard from him since.

Before Saturday, they'd talked just about every day.

"Come on, Petunia, let's get you fed," she said, forcing cheer into her tone as she took a container of chopped-up green beans from the refrigerator. The rescue macaw, the family member she'd adopted during a spread on animal abuse, used to scream on a daily basis. Now she only did so when she sensed that Jane was upset.

"Beans. Pet beans... Beans. Pet beans for Pet." The twenty-four-inch blue beauty chirped, skittering to the back of her perch and watching as Jane filled her dish. "Beans. Pet beans for Pet." As usual, Jane took an extra couple of minutes to smooth the young bird's silky feathers.

"That's right, my sweet. Pet beans for Pet," she crooned. "Mama's going to be gone for two nights," she added slowly. "One…two…pet beans for Pet while I'm gone." Sitting still while Jane touched her, Petunia eyed her full bowl. "Brad will stop by to feed you."

The bird shifted on her perch.

Petunia might understand every word. Macaws were intelligent birds. If nothing else, Jane's tone of voice had worked wonders on the bird's disposition in the two years since she'd taken her in.

"Bell!"

Petunia's screech ended their cuddling session, just a second before the doorbell rang. When Jane had first brought Petunia home she'd been horribly upset by the sound of the doorbell. Jane got in the habit of watching for her guests and saying "bell" when they approached the door. About six months later the bird had started screeching the word right before anyone rang, apparently hearing steps on the porch.

Right now, the bird's squawking didn't command Jane's full attention. The fact that Brad had rung the doorbell did that.

BRAD WAS ON THE PHONE most of the way to the airport. Business. Important business, judging by his end of the conversation.

But still business that probably could have waited another hour.

They were five minutes from the airport by the time he hung up.

"You going to be okay?" he asked, glancing over at her.

Jane tried not to stare at his hands on the steering wheel. She'd been trying—and failing—to ignore them since he'd picked her up almost forty-five minutes earlier.

Before she'd felt those strong, firm hands on her body, she'd never noticed them.

"I'm fine," she said. Who was she talking to? A lawyer who was kind to abused women? An ex-lover? Brad no longer felt like the buddy she needed.

How and when had she come to rely on him so heavily?

Brad had never been hers and never would be. She knew that. Someday he'd find the right woman and settle down. Marry. And have a wife who maybe wouldn't want a female best friend in her husband's life.

Jane was prepared for that. But in the distant future, not now when her world was cracking around her.

Brad pulled up to departing flights and climbed out to help Jane with her luggage.

Setting her carry-on down at the curb, he hesitated. "You've got your ID?"

"Of course."

"Okay, well…" His hands hung at his sides—where they belonged—and somehow managed to look awkward there. "Call me when you got there?"

That was new. But… "Sure."

"Take care."

"I will."

He turned away and then back. "I'll be waiting to hear…"

Jane nodded and walked off.

CHAPTER FIVE

Chandler, Ohio
Friday, March 26, 2010

MELANIE BONABY, MY THIRD client of the day, left my office without a smile on her face. I wasn't smiling, either. Ten o'clock in the morning and I'd already had a harrowing day. I cared deeply about Melanie. I'd gone to school with her younger sister. I used to jump on the trampoline in their backyard when I was a kid. But Melanie had quit thinking rationally a long time ago. Probably back when her mother had roughed her up as a kid.

Or maybe when Trevor Bonaby had cheated on her the first time.

Whatever the reason, I felt for her, in spite of the fact that she'd made life hell for everyone around her for years. I felt for her because, initially, she'd been a kind person and because she'd been so badly hurt. But that didn't make her current behavior healthy. She was stalking the her ex-husband. Spreading lies about him, calling the police to report illegal activities that Trevor hadn't actually done. Enough was enough. She'd divorced Trevor years before. It was time to move on. To stop obsessing over ways to make him pay.

If she didn't stop, she was going to end up in jail.

I'd just told her so.

She'd looked at me as though I was the worst kind of traitor. The kind you'd trusted with your life only to have them stab you.

I wasn't a traitor. I was a therapist. Doing my job in a small town where I knew, or know of, pretty much everyone.

There were four restaurants in town—not including all the fast-food places that had sprung up in the past decade—and I couldn't go to a single one of them without having someone stop me to tell me about a problem.

A couple of the teenage girls at church called me the fix-it lady. I guess the description fit, in one sense, but I didn't really like it. I didn't fix things; other people fixed them. I just listened and tried to give clarity if and where I could.

Five after ten. My next appointment was due in another five minutes and I'd barely looked at the file. Sheila had said earlier that I might need to interview James Todd's first wife. But she'd only called the day before, immediately after her meeting with Jane Hamilton, to confirm that I would, indeed, be adding her to my informational base for this particular project—and talking to her this morning, in fact.

Or, as Sheila put it, "She's hiding something, Kel. Get the truth out of her for me, would ya?"

I didn't bother reminding Sheila that my role was just to give opinions in court. Not to crack cases. Or people. We both knew that I'd do what I could to help.

Nine minutes past the hour, my receptionist and sometimes skating buddy buzzed me over the telephone intercom. "Ms. Hamilton is here."

"Thanks, Deb. I'll be right out."

I'd learned that Jane Hamilton was the managing

editor of *Twenty-Something,* a newish magazine that apparently covered hard-hitting issues pertinent to young adult women in addition to the usual gossip and fashion. I'd heard of it, so I figured it was reasonably successful.

Which made the woman at the helm, the woman I was to assess, a success, as well.

Wiping my hands on the sides of my navy slacks, I walked with what I hoped looked like purpose down the hall.

The waiting room, complete with two chairs and a table sporting a mishmash of dated tried-and-trues like *Time* and *Better Homes and Gardens,* had only one visitor. A woman at least three inches taller than my five-two stood there, dressed all in black, with chocolate-brown hair that curled down her back. Her purse and heels matched perfectly.

Elegance and poise personified.

Camouflage for what lay beneath? Perfect aesthetics to distract the viewer from the flawed woman they covered?

Or the clothes of a self-contained, successful woman?

"Ms. Hamilton?" I asked, extending my hand as I came through the doorway.

Deb was typing away through the half wall on the opposite side of the waiting room. And I couldn't wait to hear her first impressions of our visitor.

"I'm Kelly Chapman," I said as the woman turned to me. "Come on back."

The self-possessed smile on Ms. Hamilton's face was betrayed by the rigid set of her shoulders, the heavy steps following me down the hall.

And I had my answer about the clothes. Definitely a cover-up.

"What can you tell me about James Todd?" I asked as soon as we'd taken seats in chairs that faced each other. I noticed that she'd avoided the couch that sat across from us. I was fully armed with pad and pen, with my cup of spare pens on the table beside me. In my job it wasn't always possible to put a meeting on pause if a pen ran out of ink.

"He's smart, witty, generally kind, well liked."

Generally kind, I wrote. Wondering about Todd in *un*general circumstances.

I heard about his reputation at the university where he'd taught for fifteen years. About his willingness to help out around the house. His need to have his wife close.

And in the generic niceties, I detected the profile of a controlling man.

"How did he treat you?" I asked, about twenty minutes into the conversation.

"He never hurt me physically, if that's what you're asking. That's what Ms. Grant wants to know."

No pause. No change of intonation or body language. Was that because he really hadn't abused her? Or was it a result of years of denying a truth her mind couldn't acknowledge?

"You're sure?"

"Positive."

She left no room for me to argue. Still…

"How about emotionally?" I asked instead. "Prior to his affair, I mean."

Jane Hamilton blinked twice. She sat up. Clasped and unclasped her hands. Still, her self-possession didn't seem to waver.

Which was why her answer, when she finally gave it, surprised me.

"Yes, actually, he did."

"Tell me about that."

"Not much to tell, really," she said, retreating as quickly as she'd surfaced. "James has a very strong personality. I was fifteen years younger than him and I'd been his student. Naturally there were times when he'd get a bit overbearing in his need to have his way."

Position of authority, I wrote. And added, *Ultimate trust.*

"Overbearing how?"

"He just didn't give up. When he'd decided something was going to happen, or not happen, he wouldn't compromise."

"And if you went against him?"

"For the first couple of years of our marriage, I didn't."

"And in the three that followed?"

"He got angry."

"What did he do when he got angry?"

"He'd keep going on about whatever I'd done to upset him, throw it in my face every time I tried to talk to him about anything. Tell me what was wrong with me, blame his bad behavior on me. He wouldn't let it go."

"So he was always mad?"

"No. He went on a lot of school trips and he was always fine by the time he got back."

"He was with his other wife during those times, right?"

"Obviously, but I didn't know about the bigamy until last week."

"But you knew he was having an affair?"

"Not until the end."

Ultimate betrayal.

"Do you feel as though you owe James Todd any loyalty?" A common trait in abused women toward their abuser.

Jane Hamilton's answer would be very telling.

"No," she said after a long pause. "I don't feel any loyalty to him at all."

I was glad.

JANE HAD BEEN BACK in Allenville for more than a week and Brad had seen her only twice. Once for a trip to Chicago for the next in the series of symphony pop concerts they'd subscribed to. And the second time for a private viewing of a modern art show, a by-invitation-only preview of the work of a controversial artist featured in Jane's magazine.

Brad had been very careful to avoid physical contact of any kind. Their surroundings had prevented in-depth conversation.

Other than a brief "it was fine," she hadn't told him anything about her trip to Ohio.

But they'd talked almost every night. Long enough for him to know that protection was parked right outside her door.

She hadn't received any more messages, but the police weren't backing off at all. Not in their investigation and not in the added security measures at her workplace.

The stress was taking its toll on Jane. She hardly laughed at all these days and almost never teased him. But then, he couldn't blame the threats for that.

He and his idiot idea to "help her out" were equally to blame. There was no way he could take back the moment when he'd crossed from concerned friend to turned-on guy. No way he could make this better. Neither could he let her go. He missed Jane—needed the balance she brought to his life. And she seemed to need him, too, because she hadn't offered to give him her symphony ticket. She'd also asked him to the art show. And she'd called for another ride to the airport, too, asking him to take her just as he always had.

On the repeat trip to the airport the following Tuesday morning he stayed off the phone and tried to find a way back into the easy friendship he and Jane had shared.

Or he'd intended to try. She'd spent most of the drive on the phone with Marge Davenport, her senior editor.

"What time is your meeting?" he asked at Midway's departure curb, lifting her bag out of the trunk. She was off to Vermont to interview a couple of the legislators who were attempting to make the Missouri model— a system of small group housing, sports, school and counselors for juvenile delinquents as opposed to cell incarceration—mandatory across the United States.

Brad was on his way to court—with Kim Maplewood to defend her against the ex-husband suing her for shared custody of their only child in spite of the restraining order against him for stalking and harassment. Shawn Maplewood, the father, was alleging that since he'd never harmed his child, his ex-wife had no right to keep that child from him. Jason Maplewood, their six-year-old son, had been named in the restraining order as a member of his mother's household, and was therefore considered a protected person.

The police had questioned Shawn regarding the threats against Jane, but so far had nothing. There wasn't even enough evidence for a search warrant.

"My meeting with the senators?" Jane said, breaking into his thoughts. "Two today. And then tomorrow morning I'm at police headquarters and the juvenile jail. Juvenile court's tomorrow afternoon. And then Thursday morning I'm out in the schools, talking to teachers."

He knew her schedule. Most of their recent conversation had been centered around their work. She'd tried, once, after her trip to Chandler, to talk about them, but he hadn't engaged. He'd taken an incoming call instead He'd been afraid she was going to tell him that their friendship was no longer working for her. If he could just buy them a little time...

And since then, they'd stuck to good, safe, innocuous conversation.

It had been as though they were on hold, waiting for something. But what? The police to catch the jackass who was threatening her? The trial in Ohio? Or their friendship to die a slow, painful death?

The one thing he knew they weren't waiting for was a repeat of the insanity up on the hill in his woods. Whether he ever managed to erase the memories or not, there was no future in sleeping with Jane.

If ever there was a woman alive that he wouldn't risk hurting as deeply as he'd hurt Emily, it was Jane.

Hell, he'd done enough damage without even trying to love her.

"My plane lands at 5:50 on Thursday." Jane took the bag he'd been holding.

"I'll be here."

She was two steps away when she turned back, probably expecting him to be gone already. He wasn't. The vulnerability in her eyes called out to him so loudly he could hear nothing else. And then she smiled. A benign expression he hardly recognized.

"Don't worry about Pet," he told her, closing the

trunk. "I'll make sure she doesn't spend too much time alone."

He might even sleep on Jane's couch one night while she was gone. Just because her bird was a rescue creature and still somewhat fragile.

Jane nodded. And then he was in front of her, not sure how he'd arrived there or why. He gave her a quick, awkward hug and told her to call him each night.

He didn't stay to watch as she strode away into the terminal.

BRAD TOLD HIMSELF the dinner with Christine Ryan was business. As Jason Maplewood's attorney, also hired by Kim, Christine had been in court that morning for the custody hearing. A contentious mediation that had ended in a trial date being set.

After court, when Christine had asked Brad if he was free for dinner to talk about the case, he'd practically salivated at the chance to be out and about with an attractive woman.

To get over his obsession with Jane.

He'd quickly agreed to drive to Chicago to meet her at an upscale lawyer hangout that used to be his old stomping ground. Back when he'd had an apartment in the city and had stomped around quite frequently. Back before dates had matured into quiet dinners and nights at the theater.

He fed Pet and sat with her while she ate.

"I'm going to make it right with Jane," he explained to the wise-eyed young bird. "We've been friends too long for this to last." And when the bright blue macaw continued to assess him judgmentally, he added, "I'm going to dinner tonight. Your mama will feel less threatened by me if I'm dating."

If Jane even felt threatened. He imagined she did and his imagination was about all he had to go on these days. Jane wasn't making him privy to her feelings.

Pet picked up an orange slice and started to munch. Then spat it out.

"I didn't mean to hurt her," he told her. The bird spat again. "It just…in that moment, seeing her up there on the blanket in the grass…it felt right.…"

Petunia picked up another slice of fruit. Brad let himself out before she could spit at him a third time.

WHAT WAS IT ABOUT HOTEL ROOMS that made one feel so completely alone? Trying to contain the panic that seemed to be always threatening these days, Jane thought about calling Brad. In the old days, before the Saturday that-changed-everything, she'd have been on the phone with him the second she thought about calling. And assuming he didn't have a date, they might have talked all through dinner, too. Instead, Jane checked in and ordered salad and a glass of wine from room service.

She stood at the window, watching people scurry about in the scenic downtown square below, and told herself that she was safe. No one but Marge and Brad knew exactly where she was. She didn't have to worry about threats. She didn't have to worry about James. Or her failing friendship with Brad.

Dinner arrived and she sat down to eat.

And tried not to think. About Brad. James. Her trip to Chandler. Future trips to Chandler. The possibility of seeing her ex-husband seated at the defense table.

Seeing him in jail.

Jane shivered. She took another sip of wine and retrieved her laptop from its case.

She worked her way through another few bites of

dinner, typing up her mental and scribbled notes. She was using much of the information gleaned on this trip for her editorial that would introduce a special issue on the effectiveness of United States court systems. The rest of the magazine content would come from her staff.

Court systems. What if she really did have to testify? Face James in a courtroom? Dr. Chapman had asked if she felt any loyalty to her ex-husband. She'd said no and meant it.

But the question had been haunting her ever since. She didn't feel the least bit loyal to the man who'd betrayed her, who'd married another woman while still her husband. But what about the man she'd loved? The James who had the sensitivity to delve into ancient literature and find depths that few people had the courage to see.

How did that man promise himself, in love and loyalty, to two women at the same time? What was she missing? Why hadn't she known?

And what about Brad? Had he slept with her out of pity? Had she become another one of his charity cases, no different from his pro bono clients? Not that he ever slept with his clients. But the pro bono part... Did he see her so differently that he couldn't get beyond a few aberrant minutes and still be her friend? Had she become, God forbid, just like all of the other women he'd had sex with? Disposable to him? Didn't he know how much she needed him right now?

God, how she needed him.

Her friend. Her confidant. Not the man whose hands had moved with such assurance over her body, knowing things about her that she hadn't known about herself.

The intense physical pleasure he'd known how to arouse. The places he'd touched... It hadn't been personal. For either of them. But those moments had been memorable. So much so that they appeared in her dreams sometimes.

When she wasn't having nightmares.

Exasperated with herself, Jane opened her e-mail inbox, thankful for the convenience of wireless hookup. Clearly she had too much time on her hands. An hour spent on business communication would be far more productive. She was thirty-two, not thirteen.

Scrolling down through the one hundred and fifty new messages, Jane froze when she saw the subject line on one from her senior editor.

There'd been another threat. Hands trembling, Jane opened the e-mail from Marge Davenport.

Another anonymous note had come to the office that day—nearly two weeks after the last one. Marge said she'd tried to call, but when she hadn't been able to get through, she'd scanned the note and sent it electronically as she did everything she thought Jane would want immediately.

Detective Thomas had already picked up the original. There'd been no other unusual activity in the *Twenty-Something* offices, and nothing in the building, either.

The note was generic. Grammar unremarkable. Punctuation normal. But it stood out starkly because it was different from the first three.

You can't afford a screwup. Too much is at stake. You know what's right. Do it.

Jane didn't reply to her editor.

She called room service for another glass of wine, but found it tasteless. She poured it down the sink and left the empty glass with the rest of her tray outside her door.

And at eight o'clock, when the room's quiet was more than she could bear, she phoned Brad.

He didn't pick up.

RETURNING TO HIS OLD HANGOUT probably hadn't been a great choice. Standing at the sink in the men's restroom a little past ten, Brad thought about the hour's drive home. He was going to have to get a hotel room in the city. He wasn't drunk by any stretch, but he'd had enough to drink to forget about the people he'd hurt. And to concentrate on the woman he was with. Christine Ryan wasn't the type of woman to fall head over heels for anyone.

Which made her perfect for Brad.

He dried his hands, and just before heading back out into less private territory, checked his cell phone. He'd asked Jane to call and she had. Three times.

He quickly opened a text box and started typing.

Fed Pet. Having dinner in the city with attorney on case. Sleep well. Be safe. Talk to you tomorrow.

Then he turned off his phone.

How can I sleep well without talking to you first?
I got another threat.

Lying in bed, Jane hit the delete key on her phone. No guilt.

Which case?

Delete again. Like she was checking up on him?

Who's the attorney? Do I know him?

She watched the cursor erase those words, as well.

Brad had avoided conversation with her, damn him. She needed him tonight.

At least he hadn't ignored her completely. No matter who he was with, he'd taken the time to text her. He'd been thinking about her. But how could he not be thinking of her? She'd been ringing his phone all night. Which wasn't like her.

Is this it, then? The blow off?

Another pause while the cursor made letters vanish.

I got another note.

She was right back where she started. And deleted again. She wasn't going to play the sympathy card. Her stalker would have no way of knowing she was in Vermont. She was perfectly safe here. Away, just as Detective Thomas wanted.

Besides, if Brad didn't care enough to call, she wasn't going to tell him about her troubles.

Are you going to sleep with her?

Erase. Erase. Erase.

So what if he ran those hands down another woman's body? That was inevitable.

Jane had liked things a lot better when she hadn't known what the woman on the receiving end of Brad's attentions was actually getting.

Sniffling, Jane waited until her eyes, blurred over with tears, cleared enough for her to see.

She was being an idiot. Acting like someone from the young end of her readership. This wasn't high school. This was life.

She didn't want to be Brad's lover. As great as he was at sex, she needed his friendship more. He didn't mix the two. And she wasn't in any state to even try to trust another man with her heart. She was way too confused. About the past. James. Her culpability in trusting a man who'd been married to another woman—in being a young wife who couldn't satisfy her husband.

And she was afraid, too.

About the past. James. Her culpability.

And about the present. Her stalker. What he wanted. And what he was going to take from her if she didn't comply.

Be careful driving home.

Jane read, re-read, then sent. She set the phone beside her pillow, turned out the light and ordered herself to sleep.

Instead, she lay wide-eyed in the dark, thought about her marriage, the infidelities that had transpired when she hadn't been able to give James what he needed and wanted, and noticed that Brad didn't reply.

CHAPTER SIX

"You know how I feel about Jason's well-being," Brad said, leaning forward at the table so his auburn-haired companion could hear him. "But I'm just not convinced that every child needs both parents, certainly not enough to set precedent like you're suggesting."

"We've got a six-year-old boy who misses his dad. He's so far unaware of the damage his father has done. I just think the law should be changed regarding members of household in a restraining order when one of the members is a child whose restrained parent has visiting rights. Assuming the parent has never harmed the child in any way."

"I get that. And in theory, I can see what you're saying. But Kim hired you…"

"To protect Jason. Because she loves her son enough to admit that she isn't sure she's seeing things clearly where he's concerned and she wants to do what's best for him."

"The man has made Kim's life hell. He's written to her employers and people she works with, telling lies about her, discrediting her. He's followed her, nearly driving her off the road."

"There was no proof of that and Jason wasn't in the car."

"He called and e-mailed, many times a day, berating her, telling her what a horrible person she is to taunt her into mental submission. He called her family. All of her friends, spreading vicious rumors. This in addition to backhanding her. The man is cruel."

"He was put on probation for slapping her and according to Kim, he was a wonderful father."

"Because Jason hasn't disappointed him yet."

"Maybe. Or maybe Shawn really loved his wife and is having a hard time handling their divorce. The darker side to a great passion."

"He threatened her life," Brad said. This was the same conversation they'd been having all night. A conversation that was engaging his attention. And still, when Christine turned to speak to a fellow attorney who'd stopped at their table, Brad thought of Jane, wondering if she was in her hotel room, wondering if she was alone. She'd never brought anyone to her hotel room before, but now that he'd reawakened her sexuality...

"Shawn has never threatened his son or hurt him in any way." Christine had turned back. "Exactly the opposite. Shawn spent much of his time with his son. Teaching him, taking him to church. With Jason, he has the patience of a saint. And Jason started to cry when he told me how much he misses his dad. They used to go fishing. Shawn was helping him learn to catch. The boy seems to think, watch and dream baseball—something Kim knows nothing about." Christine continued, her eyes full of life and passion as she advocated for her client.

"The court found the man dangerous enough to keep him away from Kim. It's not for us to determine when and how he's dangerous."

"I'm not talking about arbitrarily and automatically excluding kids from parental restraining orders, but I think that, in this case, an exception needs to be made so that Shawn has some kind of window of opportunity for at least supervised visitation rights."

Brad thought of Kim's reduced income. The bills she had piling up as a result of her divorce.

"Mrs. Maplewood would have to foot the bill for motions made on Jason's behalf. She could go bankrupt over this."

"Not if a couple of us share the workload and can then afford to offer our services pro bono."

Christine's piercing green eyes looked straight at him without blinking.

"You want me to join with you," he said slowly. "You want us to do this together."

Together. Him and her. A case he believed in. People he cared about. And a woman who could distract him from missing Jane.

"I've seen you work, Brad. I've seen a lot of attorneys work and no one stands out like you do. Nothing slips by you. Not a blink, a shudder or a misquoted law. You have this uncanny ability to pull all truth and right out of any hat. And you care. I've watched you with Mrs. Maplewood. You'd do anything within your legal power to help that woman and her son. If you don't like what I'm suggesting, then join me. Together we can find the right solution here."

"I'd do anything in my power to help any of my clients." Brad just wanted that known. This case was important, but no more so and no less than any other case.

"Yeah, me, too." Christine's tone softened almost imperceptibly. But as she'd just pointed out, Brad noticed things. "I think with you on my team, I can't go wrong."

She was talking about the case. There was no doubt about that.

But, unless Brad had lost all discernment, Christine was offering more, too. In such a way that she wouldn't lose face if he turned her down.

"It's what Kim wants—to give her son the best chance, whether she agrees with the means or not. She knows you're fighting for her. She wants me to fight for Jason. But it would be much easier for everyone if you were with us."

"Can I think about this?" He knew the words were the right ones. Knew, too, that she would take them for the affirmative they were probably going to be.

Her warm smile gave her away. "Of course. I can wait a day or two. Have another drink with me?"

Brad thought about calling a cab. He thought about the mess he'd recently made of his life. The risk of increasing the damage by hurting Jane further. And nodded.

"Hi."

"Hi."

Standing at the bathroom mirror in her hotel room, Jane saw the trembling in her hand as she held her phone to her ear. That scared her. She was letting things get to her and that had to stop.

"Are you alone?" She couldn't talk to Brad comfortably if he had someone in bed with him. Or sharing breakfast with him.

"Of course."

A piece of her heart settled back into place. She felt calmer, which made no sense.

Her hair was curled, soft and natural-looking around her shoulders and beyond. Her pink linen suit pressed. Accessories understated yet noticeable. Makeup tasteful.

She'd be ready to face the long day if she hadn't spent the night awake.

She thought about telling Brad about the escalated threat. She'd already been on the phone with Thomas that morning.

The police were trying to get DNA from the envelope flaps, but so far, had had no luck.

"Are you home?" Jane cringed, afraid she sounded like she was checking up on him.

"No. I had a couple of drinks so I got a room here instead of driving home."

"What about your attorney friend? Did he get a room, too?"

"No."

She had to stop. She was making matters worse by putting pressure on a relationship that couldn't take any more.

"And it wasn't a he. I had dinner with Christine Ryan."

Her hair still looked fine. Her makeup tasteful. She was falling apart and it didn't show.

"Kim's new attorney for Jason?"

"Yes."

In the olden days, he'd have told her all about the evening.

"She asked me to share the case with her, pro bono. I'm going to do it."

So he was going to see her again. Work with her. Sleep with her.

She meant to tell Brad about the newest threat. That was why she'd called. And said, "Oh, good. I just noticed the time. I'm going to be late. I'll call you tonight."

With that, she went out to face another day.

BRAD SPENT MUCH of Wednesday immersing himself in work. And when he had a free minute, he occupied it with Jason Maplewood's case, doing his own statistical research. He thought about Jane a time or two, hoping she was faring well. Glad to have her out of the city and out of danger.

The new case inspired him. Like he'd been inspired when he'd been fresh out of law school and convinced he could change the world. Back before he'd lived in the real world long enough to know that nothing was exactly as it seemed.

And winning wasn't always right.

He and Jane had to make things right somehow. That was all there was to it. He'd screwed up. Betrayed her trust by telling her that he was going to help her, and then mounting her like a rutting bull.

Fifteen minutes couldn't wipe out a friendship. Could it? He and Jane needed each other, so he had to make room for their friendship to flower again. And the only way to do that was to obliterate the sex. He had to get himself firmly involved with someone else.

So maybe he was also interested in Jason's case because Christine Ryan was an interesting woman.

On his way into the city to pick up Jane at the airport on Thursday evening he switched on his Bluetooth and gave the voice command for Christine. His suit coat hung on the hook behind him. His tie was loose and his top button undone. He was officially finished working for the day.

"I'm in," he said as soon as she picked up.

"Great! So when do we get started? I'm writing the brief the judge requested and could use some help. I think it would help if we know about every custody ruling that's happened in this state in the past year or so. And other states, too, if we can get to them."

"Let's get the brief done first and see where that leads us, thoughtwise." It could be a couple of months before their next court date but they didn't need to wait for an answer before trying something else.

"I have a folder of cases. There was one in Florida last year. A nine-year-old boy…"

Brad listened and they brainstormed as he drove. Noticing the passing road signs, he was shocked to see the airport exit up ahead. Where had forty-five minutes gone?

"Can you meet me in the city tonight?" Christine asked when he told her he had to go. "We can meet at my place. Or at my office, I suppose, but I have the Maplewood files at home since I was planning to continue pro bono."

"With or without my help?"

"Yes. But I'm very glad you've decided to join me. Something tells me we could be good together."

"I'm busy tonight," he told her, a bit of a smile on his face. He wasn't ready to rush into bed with her. A little anticipation was nice. As was testing the waters to make certain that anything that might happen between them would be reciprocally no heartstrings attached. "How about Saturday morning?"

"Nine o'clock?"

"I'll bring bagels."

Christine promised to e-mail him her address and they rang off. Brad pulled up next to the airport terminal with his mind cleared of everything but fixing his relationship with Jane.

CHAPTER SEVEN

JANE WAS SURPRISED when Brad asked her to dinner. She'd been prepared for him to be on the phone the entire drive and had notes in her purse that she'd planned to review in the car.

And work to do when she got home. The three days away had put her behind on her responsibilities.

"I'd rather just get home," she said as they merged into Chicago rush-hour traffic. "I'm really tired."

That was an understatement. She'd done a lot of hard thinking about a lot of things.

"Was the trip a success?" Brad's phone remained clipped to his black leather belt.

"I got what I went for," she told him, meaning the words in more ways than one. She'd found clarity in Vermont about their friendship. She didn't go into that, though, taking the safer route of sharing with him the conditions she'd found at the juvenile detention center she'd visited.

"I hate that we live in a society that locks up juvenile offenders in prisons where they are often beaten, where sex runs rampant, where rape occurs and then, when they turn eighteen we just set them loose. We create animals and then expect them, because they have a birthday, to suddenly emerge as respectable adults," Jane said, longing for a soak in her Jacuzzi tub after she sat with Pet for a bit.

Longing for that dinner Brad had suggested. Longing for things to be as they once were between them.

She stared straight ahead, at the license plates in front of them, the varying shades of red brake lights. Brad's long legs, his hands mastering the steering wheel were his business. Not hers.

"Keeping children innocent and protected seems to be a thing of the past," she continued, focusing on what mattered. "We've got fourteen-year-olds having sex in jail, and those with the ability to do something about it throw up their hands and say they can't stop them."

Oh, God. Why couldn't she get sex off the brain when she was with Brad? There were a lot of other things about juvenile detention that she could have mentioned in her attempt to face normalcy.

"And are you going to print that sentiment?"

"I don't know," she said. "This is much bigger than how we rehabilitate problem kids, isn't it? They're growing up so much more quickly. The crimes they're committing are so much more…adult in nature. And their actions in detention are, as well. Instead of crying at night, they're having orgies. The Internet has made everything so much more accessible to them."

"Maybe things are different and maybe they're not. Maybe the crimes were always being committed," Brad offered. "Maybe it's just that now, with technology and the Internet making it all so much more public, we're finding out what kids were doing anyway."

Jane was shocked. "You think kids have always been having sex before they even reach puberty?"

"I don't know."

The sudden silence gave lie to the pretence. They couldn't go back, couldn't have normal conversations.

The sex was between them now, forcing itself in one way or another.

"I was sixteen the first time I saw a naked woman—and then it was only breasts."

Brad's words were like bricks breaking glass. What was he doing? Jane didn't know what to say. She needed to escape. And wanted to know what he was telling her, too. Even though she shouldn't.

"I was seventeen the first time I had sex," he continued after a minute, almost defensively, as though he knew the conversation was charged but he was going to have it anyway. "The summer after high school graduation."

"Who was she?" *Shut up, Jane. What does it matter?*

"A girl I met at work. She was older—twenty-one. Her boyfriend had just ditched her. We hung out all summer. She taught me a lot."

Jane hated the woman. "What happened to her?"

"I have no idea," Brad said. "I left for college in the fall and never saw her again."

"She didn't try to get in touch with you?"

"No, we knew the score from the beginning. I was just a kid to her. A balm to her bruised spirits."

"And what about you? What was she to you?"

Maybe he was right. Maybe this was how they got their friendship back—by just jumping right into the fire. Not running or avoiding or pretending. Sex existed. They'd had it.

"Truthfully?" He glanced over at her.

"Yes."

Eyes back on the traffic, his voice was soft as he said, "She was my own personal angel. I knew there was no way we'd ever be a couple, not in the real world, but I was still crushed when, a few weeks before I left, she started seeing some guy she'd met at a club."

"It might have been kinder for her to wait until after you'd left."

"Or maybe this was the kindest way. She sent me off free and clear, with no reason to look back."

She wanted the awkwardness gone between them. Needed his friendship.

"What about you? When was your first time?" If casually talking about their sex lives could help...

"The first time I saw a naked man was on my wedding night."

James had had to marry her for her to sleep with him. Brad hadn't even had to date her.

The thought just confirmed the conclusion Jane had reached in Vermont.

Sex was with them now.

They'd ruined everything.

"HAVE YOU HEARD ANY MORE from Ohio?" Brad asked when his body started to react. Acknowledging the elephant in the room wasn't working. It was only making the problems worse.

She'd been a virgin when she'd married James. And hadn't experienced sexual feelings since. Did that mean he'd been only her second lover?

"No. I'm still waiting on a call from Ms. Grant with a date for my deposition." Wearing navy dress slacks and a matching jacket, Jane looked every bit the capable, successful woman as she sat in the passenger seat of his BMW. There was no trace of the woman who'd confided in him that Saturday on the blanket in the woods.

"And nothing new from Detective Thomas?"

"Not today."

Not today? "Have you spoken to him since you've been gone?"

"Yesterday." She stared straight ahead. "Another letter arrived on Tuesday."

And she was only now telling him? "The same as before?"

"The delivery and physical appearance were the same. The message was a little different."

All senses on alert, he glanced her way. "Different how?"

"'You can't afford a screwup. Too much is at stake. You know what's right. Do it,'" she quoted.

It had to stop. The threats. This tension between him and Jane. All of it.

"It's escalating."

"Yep."

"What does Thomas say?"

"He wants me to work from home."

"Are you going to?"

"I will when I can, but if these threats are about the magazine, I have to be there. I'm not going to leave my staff in danger without me."

"Or you might be putting them in danger by being there. No one else is getting mail, right?"

"Right. But we still don't know if the threats are coming to me personally, or just because I'm in charge. As a compromise, I'm going to vary my hours from day to day. Changing my routine so that I'm not predictable. Take different routes to work, park in different places."

Brad didn't like it. Not any of it. The threats. The changes. The danger...

"When were you going to tell me?"

He waited, half-afraid of her answer. And when she

said nothing, Brad pushed his foot to the accelerator. Time to stop cruising.

"We have to fix us, Jane. We have to talk about it. Yell at me, blame me, do whatever it takes to get this wedge out from between us. We're losing something great.

"I promise you, I won't touch you again. I can't risk hurting you like I hurt Emily. I'd rather die than do that. You're perfectly safe. If anything, you're safer than ever because I know how much is at stake."

She still wasn't talking. If she needed more convincing, that was fine. He could convince forever. He believed in his cause—in them—that strongly. "Come on. We can do this. We can make it work."

"It's too late, Brad."

"Sex isn't worth losing you."

"I guess we should have thought of that before we took our pants off."

"We put them back on. We're both determined to keep them on " A thought occurred to him, hitting him like the headlights from the opposite lane. "Aren't we?"

Jane didn't flinch or even look his way. "If you're asking me if I want to sleep with you again, the answer is no." There was no defensiveness in her tone, just calm fact. At least that was what he was getting.

That and a sick feeling in his gut.

"I can't have sex again without a committed relationship and aside from the fact that you aren't interested, there's no way I could even consider starting one right now. It would be emotional suicide. And a lie."

"A lie?"

"How can I promise my heart to someone else when I don't even trust it myself? I need to get through this situation with James. And I need to focus on these threats and hopefully figure out who's sending them or what it is I'm supposed to do. Beyond that, I've got a magazine to run. I'm fully tapped, Brad. I can't afford to split my energy any further."

"Sounds like you need a friend. A shoulder to lean on."

"Maybe I do." Her quiet voice in his car soothed him, until she continued. "But it can't be you. Not anymore."

"Why not?" Sex didn't have to mean anything. He was completely sure about that.

"Because I'm not you." She took a deep breath. "I can't erase the fact that we were intimate. I can't pretend, every time I look at your hands, that I don't know what they feel like touching me. I can't look at you in your work clothes and pretend that I don't know what's under them. And I can't cover back up because you've seen me."

When she finally turned her head, Brad saw the resolution in her eyes. And knew he'd lost.

CHAPTER EIGHT

JANE WAITED A WEEK to fall apart. First, she looked up Christine Ryan in a legal directory and arranged an interview with her for *Twenty-Something*'s justice system issue, telling herself that, as an attorney who specialized in representing juveniles, the woman had insight pertinent to Jane's article for the special edition.

And she was fully cognizant that there was more to the invitation than professional interest. She had to meet the woman who was most likely the current recipient of Brad's particular skills. She had to accept the fact that he wasn't hers—and move on.

Jane had to face what she'd done. Had to face the fact that she'd allowed a man to touch her intimately, without love and commitment. Without any hope of a future relationship.

She wasn't going to hide from anyone. Nor from the pain she'd incurred from having sex with Brad and not from the loneliness left by his absence in her life.

She left a message for Brad, as a courtesy, informing him of the impending Monday-morning coffee meeting between his ex-best friend and the new woman in his life.

She didn't invite him.

And was glad that she hadn't when, with security shadow in tow, she met the attorney at the upscale beanery down the street from her office that next breezy, gray Monday morning. Christine was worse than she'd imagined. Slender in all the right places and not so slender where it counted. Her hair had hints of auburn and curled easily around her shoulders. Her suit was expensive and fit her as though it had been designed for her body. Loose enough to be professional, but snug enough to move with her. Her shirt, while not tight, did nothing to camouflage the generous proportions of her breasts.

They were probably real, too.

"Thanks for meeting with me," Jane said as they waited in line to order their coffees.

"I'm thrilled you called." Christine's smile seemed genuine. "Really. I've read your magazine. It's classy, to the point, honest. You aren't afraid to tackle tough issues. I'm honored that you think I have something to say worth writing about." They moved up a couple of spaces in a line of twenty or so.

An hour later, Jane was still at the coffee shop, her caramel latte a thing of the distant past. The notepad in front of her was overflowing. Walt Overmeyer, sitting alone at the table behind her, was on his third cup of coffee. Jane didn't know if he was drinking them to stay awake on such a boring job or if he was merely pretending so he didn't look as conspicuous.

Whatever the case, she'd grown used to the man and was glad to have him there.

"The Missouri model for juvenile offenders outlines a more secure and supportive home life environment than many kids are given. Especially those from lower-income areas, which, statistically, produce many of our juvenile offenders. The type of incarceration you describe would be more of a reward than a punishment." The beautiful attorney sat forward, vibrating with passion for the topic. Jane wondered if she felt similar passion for Brad.

Jane cared about the topic, too. And didn't want to feel passion for Brad.

"So we might make society safer on the back end, when these offenders are released, but we could be increasing initial crime."

Christine frowned and still looked gorgeous. "Possibly. But statistics also point to the success of the scared straight philosophy." Sitting back, Christine said, "There are no easy answers, are there?"

"I haven't found any." For anything. "If you don't mind my asking, what's your personal opinion on all of this? Statistics aside, do you think it's right that convicted juvenile felons be given a break, that state money is spent on putting them in family-type facilities where they go to school and have regular counseling, play sports and musical instruments, while often non-felon kids aren't given the same support and opportunity?"

Christine's grin was more wry than humorous. "I'm not here to set forth some moral standard for society. I just know that I'd prefer to see a kid—any kid—have a chance to turn his life around rather than be forced to endure years of abuse. I'd rather those kids be rehabilitated than treated like animals and then, at eighteen, set loose on an unsuspecting society."

"You really care about what you do, don't you?"

"Yeah. I really do."

Of course she did. She was a goddess. She had to be to attract Brad's attention. So what did that make Jane? It had taken Brad two years to kiss her—and then he'd sworn her off forever. Because to him sex was impersonal and Jane was far too important to him? Or because she just didn't do it for him?

And what the hell did it matter?

"I care, too," Jane said, knowing even if Christine didn't that she was speaking about far more than the kids they were discussing. "I'd just rather see more money going into programs to deter juvenile offenders from the outset, if that's possible...."

"You sound a lot like someone else I know."

Christine couldn't be referring to Brad. That possibility was only presenting itself because Jane had been trying her best—and failing miserably—not to think about him spending all of his free time with this woman.

Christine's glance changed. Her whole demeanor softened—as though they'd switched from being two professionals to two women. Jane had dressed her part in designer slacks, jacket and her one pair of three-hundred-dollar shoes. She was working, in control and sure of herself. Even so, the other woman's gaze unsettled her.

"I've been trying to figure out a way to bring Brad Manchester into the conversation," Christine said.

"Brad? Why?" Jane burned inside. She'd been found out.

"You and he used to be an item, didn't you?"

"No." Jane had no problem with that answer. It wasn't the first time she'd fielded the question. "We're friends. That's all we've ever been."

"I just formally met Brad recently, when I went to court on Jason's behalf. But I've known who he was for a long time. He told me that you were the one who referred Kim Maplewood to him."

"That's right."

"I know I've seen you around together, and I just

thought, the way his voice changed when he mentioned you..."

Jane kept her expression professional. Did the other woman know that Jane had been obsessing about her and Brad for the past hour? The past week?

"Look, I don't take other women's men." Christine leaned forward. "Not interested in the karma that would come back at me. If Brad's out of line here..."

"No!" It was the truth. So why the phrase "what doesn't kill you makes you stronger" sprang to mind she had no idea. "Brad and I really are just friends. We've gone to functions together on occasion, but that's all. There's never been anything romantic between us at all." They'd gotten physical once, as a medicinal remedy. But that definitely hadn't been romantic.

"Well, good, then." Christine smiled. "We women have to stick together, you know?"

Nodding, Jane hated that she had intimate knowledge of the sexual pleasures Christine Ryan must be experiencing, but she was impressed with her as a person. Hell, the attorney was damned near perfect.

She'd made a huge mistake calling Christine. Meeting her hadn't helped. She'd just given herself a more concrete vision of Brad with another woman instead of the abstract one she'd been fighting.

"How do you do it?"

"Do what?"

"Stay immune to him?"

How would Jane have answered that question a month ago? "We've just always had more fun being friends." Not a great answer, but it was the best she could do. "Listen," she said, standing. "I really appreciate your coming down to meet with me. I'll send you a copy of the article if you'd like, before I send it to print."

"That'd be great." Christine stood as well, five feet six inches of beauty and brains—and decency.

Jane shook the other woman's hand and, with Walt in tow, made her escape.

Inside, she wanted to puke.

JANE WAS LEAVING TOWN in the morning. Sitting at his desk on Thursday, a week and six days since he'd lost the best friend he'd ever had, Brad stared out the wall of windows to his left to the street below. Whoever had said that living in the suburbs got you away from city traffic hadn't lived in a Chicago suburb.

He lived with traffic. It was a forty-five-minute commute to and from the airport or any other meeting he might have in the city.

He'd worked with Christine four of the past seven nights. They had done nothing but argue cases back and forth all week. It reminded him of his law school days.

They were trying to make a difference in one boy's life. A difference that, with a court ruling, could affect similar cases across the country.

They could be on their way to making history.

If they could agree on a recommendation that would do what they each needed it to do. They were getting close.

Jane was on her way back to Chandler, Ohio, to give a formal deposition against her ex-husband. To be reminded of how much the bastard had hurt her. How horribly her own judgment had betrayed her.

Brad would have liked to have the right to accompany her and to offer his support. To sit in the courtroom with her and try to give her strength.

Growing a little tired of all the thinking, Brad

grabbed his cell phone and pushed the first speed dial. He really should reprogram the damn thing.

"Hello?"

"Hi."

"What's up? Is something wrong?"

Other than the fact that he needed to be her friend even if she didn't want him to be? "I'd like to take you to the airport in the morning. If you haven't made other arrangements."

"That's not necessary. Walt can take me."

Why the idea made him peevish he didn't know.

"I always see you off. Wish you a safe trip."

"Now you don't have to."

"Your trip isn't going to be easy, Jane. At least let me give you a good send-off."

There was a pause and Brad worked on his next argument. He wasn't giving up on this one. He couldn't.

"Okay."

Oh. Well, good, then.

"And I'll watch Pet while you're gone, too," he added while she was in a giving frame of mind. "There's no need to upset her by having a stranger in her space, especially with you not there."

"That would be nice. Thank you."

Nice. Thank you.

"Okay then, I'll see you in the morning...."

They arranged a time and she went back to work. She'd said she had people waiting outside her office. Which could explain why she'd been so polite. But he knew better. Just like that, she was becoming a stranger to him.

He wouldn't have thought it possible.

CHAPTER NINE

TAKING A DEEP BREATH after ending the call, Jane straightened her shoulders and opened her office door.

"Sam, Donna, come on in."

The two, standing as far apart as they could in the reception room outside her office, turned and followed her inside.

"Have a seat." She motioned to the lush mauve couch along the wall, settling into one of the two matching armchairs on the other side of the solid cherry coffee table, and watched as Sam and Donna eyed each other before dropping to opposite ends of the couch.

Jane's head hurt. Probably a result of having skipped lunch. And she needed these two artists—who worked on many of the same projects—to learn to be civil to each other.

"Okay, here's how it goes." She looked between the two, her expression serious, solid and unbending. If only her stomach would take the hint. "Sam, I don't give a damn if you're gay or if anyone else is. Donna, I have no interest in your opinion of gays, gay marriage or gay rights."

The surprised expressions staring back at her were identical. They knew her well, these two. As did most of her staff. They'd all been in this venture together from the beginning. Taking on the risk of failing in a relatively small industry for the chance to do something big. Turnover was rare at *Twenty-Something*. As were times when Jane spoke without listening first.

"What you each do or don't do, believe or don't believe, outside your work, doesn't concern me. Nor does it belong here. Donna, Sam is the best writer I've ever known. Sam, Donna is a truly gifted photographer. And neither of you, if you can't find a way to work together without making everyone around you tense, will be calling this place home for much longer. Do I make myself clear?"

Sam claimed that Donna didn't respect him because his life partner was male. That she talked down to him and degraded him every chance she got. Donna claimed that Sam flaunted his lifestyle. That he talked to his partner several times a day in a voice so loud the entire floor could hear him. She also claimed that he expected preferential treatment because he was gay, though, as far as Jane knew, the only concession Sam had ever asked for was the right to bring his partner to spouses-only functions. Personally, Jane thought they were both prima donnas. She could forgive it to a point since they were both incredibly talented.

And a bit too spoiled apparently.

"Neither of you have a response?" Jane broke the thick silence that had permeated the room.

Donna was the first to answer. "What do you want us to say?"

"'Yes, ma'am,' would be a good start." Their mouths literally dropped open at her response. No one called her ma'am in these offices. Ever.

"Listen, guys," she said, leaning forward with her arms resting on the thighs of her gray slacks. "I'd hate to lose either one of you, but you're affecting the entire staff. I'm sorry you don't see eye to eye on some life issues, but unless it's a professional matter, it doesn't belong here. I can't have the magazine suffer because two of my star employees can't control their personal opinions. Honestly, the two of you are acting like children."

Sam looked down.

And then Donna did the same. "Sorry."

"Sorry doesn't do it. We need a fix. Do either of you have a suggestion?"

"What have you got against gays?" Sam asked with more than a touch of belligerence.

"My ex-husband left me for a man. A writer like you," Donna snapped, and then immediately apologized. "I'm sorry. I just… I didn't realize that I was still so angry. Or that I was taking it out on you. For Jane to have noticed, things must have gotten pretty bad."

"Yeah, well, I gotta admit, after a while I was doing everything I could to throw Lyle in your face."

"Fine," Jane interjected. "So where do we go from here?"

"We learn to play nice." Sam looked at Jane. "I'm not going to lose this job."

Nodding, Donna said, "I'm not, either. Unless it's work-related, I'll keep my opinions to myself."

Satisfied, Jane stood. And her stomach turned. "Then get out there and get to work," she said, hoping her smile took the sting out of the words. "We have an issue to produce."

"Sure thing." Sam stood, and then added, "You okay? You seem a little pale."

"Yeah, I was thinking the same thing," Donna agreed.

"Just stressed. I'm out of town again tomorrow and the juvenile delinquent editorial isn't finished yet."

Because every time she thought about working on it an image of Brad and Christine came to mind and she turned her attention to other pressing matters—like Donna and Sam. Financial plans. Fiscal budgets. The fall fashion issue. And the newest threat. It had just come that morning, telling her that time was running out. For her. This time the note had been person specific, and Jane was now afraid to go to the bathroom unescorted.

"I'm free after work," Donna said. "We could meet downstairs for a drink."

"Can I take a rain check on that?" Jane asked. "I've got planning and packing to do."

"You going back to Vermont? Need any photos? I could come along." Everyone knew about the threats, and no one was letting her go anywhere alone.

"No." Jane moved behind her desk. "It's a personal issue. I'll be home tomorrow night."

And then, depending on how valuable her testimony was to the prosecutor, she could have to go back again later for the trial.

"Something wrong?" Sam asked, stepping forward.

On another day, Jane might have told them both. But probably not. No matter how much her staff was like family to her, there were some parts of her life she needed to keep to herself.

"Nothing I can't handle," she said, wishing she was as sure on the inside as she sounded on the outside.

"It doesn't have to do with the threats, does it?"

"No." Thank God for that. At least in Chandler she'd feel safe. Sort of.

Or maybe it was just that it would be a relief to change fears.

"I haven't seen Brad around in a while," Sam pressed.

"Everything okay there?" His expression was so sweet and caring. It gave Jane's heart the push it needed.

"Everything's fine," she said. "He's busy on a tough case so we haven't had time for our usual lunches."

It was all true.

Unfortunately there were other things that were true, as well. But before Jane could get lost in that thought she had to excuse herself.

She barely made it to the ladies' room in time to throw up.

Donna, who was waiting just inside the door, pretended not to notice.

CHAPTER TEN

Friday, April 23, 2010
Chandler, Ohio

I, KELLY ANN CHAPMAN, have been sworn in at more depositions than I can count. Even if I'm just there to observe the proceedings, I have to take an oath to tell the truth. Who knows when I might inadvertently open my mouth? Or be called upon to speak—which was more likely the case. Generally I didn't have trouble keeping quiet. That came with the territory of being one who was paid to listen, I suspect. Or being the daughter of a druggie.

In any case, I had faults, but speaking out of turn wasn't one of them. I also had a headache that morning. Too much sleep maybe. Or, more likely, not enough.

I was sitting at the table in Sheila's office waiting for yet another deposition to begin, trying not to look too present. I was there as a spy and I wasn't really fond of the role. Working with the intricacies and depths of people's minds was my love. I didn't love it when I was doing so without their consent.

However, a murder had been committed. Probably by a man who, if not convicted, would repeat the performance someday—if wife number three ever got wise and wanted to move on.

I was there to help save lives.

Maybe even Ms. Hamilton's. My previous meeting with her had ended with the understanding that I wasn't needed. So why couldn't I get the self-possessed woman out of my mind?

"You remember Dr. Chapman?" Sheila said, nodding toward my end of the conference table.

"Yes." Jane Hamilton smiled that pleasant, compassionate, fully-in-control smile that left me empty.

Sheila firmly believed that Ms. Hamilton was hiding something and I agreed with her. Which meant that I was there to officially find out what.

Personally, something about the woman called out to me even though I'd spent less than an hour with her. Could be because Sheila kept pestering me about her. Not that she'd tell Ms. Hamilton, but if Sheila didn't get something out of her, she could lose this case.

James Todd, a man I'd yet to meet, seemed to be a slick one. With his third wife's money he'd hired one of the best defense attorneys in the state. They were claiming that Lee Anne Todd had killed herself. All they'd had to do was find out about the antidepressants she'd been taking and they'd practically been guaranteed success in their quest to plant doubt in the jurors' minds. That's all it took to buy a guy's freedom these days. Enough reasonable doubt.

Sheila asked all the rote questions for the record. Name, age, birth dates, both hers and the defendant's, relation to the defendant, date of marriage, date of divorce. Todd's lawyer, Sanders Elliot, took copious notes, as though this was rocket science and not readily available information from several sources, which made me wonder about him. But then, I wonder about everyone. That's my job.

Ms. Hamilton recited the details of her marriage to

James Todd. How they started out gloriously happy, discounting the usual adjustments of newlyweds setting up daily routines.

I wondered about that, too. I've worked with a lot of divorced women over the years and almost all of them describe the early days as glorious.

By the time the first ex-Mrs. Todd had reached the point in her testimony where she found out about Lee Anne, explaining that, until Sheila had called her, she'd thought her husband had simply had an affair with the other woman, I was certain something was wrong. When she'd first discovered the affair, Jane Hamilton had tried to work things out with the jerk.

Okay. Some women were that forgiving.

But suddenly, Jane had divorced him though she hadn't known about the bigamy.

So why? That's what I wanted to ask. Why didn't she want to work things out anymore?

Had the man chosen Lee Anne over her as he would later choose Marla over Lee Anne? Was he the one who'd wanted the divorce?

She'd said, three times that I knew of, that the decision to divorce had been mutual.

I didn't want to call this soft-spoken, obviously successful woman a liar, but I didn't believe her. Her eyes were too vacant.

"Did James Todd have a temper?" Sheila's questions grew more critical, more minutely to the point. As was her way. Lure the prey in, and then, slowly suck her up. I understood it. I just didn't like seeing it. Lure and conquer wasn't my way.

"No more so than other people I knew."

Odd way to put that. But that could just be the woman. It'd been a long time since I'd seen someone who weighed every word as carefully as Jane Hamilton appeared to do.

"Did you ever witness him damaging property? Did he ever break anything around your home?"

"Not intentionally."

"Could you explain that?"

"He knocked a glass off the table once and it broke. I bumped into a plate on the edge of my counter at home a few weeks ago. It broke, too. That's what I meant."

Uh-huh. I tried not to watch the woman like a hawk. But I would have liked to get her alone again, to talk to her one-on-one just to let her know that I was on her side.

I wanted to help but helping her wasn't what I was there to do.

"Did he ever hurt you?"

"Of course he did. We're divorced. He was unfaithful to me." All this was said in the same calm, assured tone.

"I meant physically. Did he ever hurt you physically?"

"He dropped a weight on my foot. We were cleaning out the spare closet and I'd been standing beside him and bumped him just as he was turning with the weight."

"Is that it? Were there any other times when he hurt you? Physically?"

"He broke my nose once."

Sheila's eyes shot open. Sanders slid down in his seat. I chafed for a notepad.

"We were playing tennis and collided on the court. He rushed me to the hospital and took quite a grilling from the resident over it. And later from our friends at the club, too. And if you're referring to the police reports, I fell down the stairs once, but James wasn't responsible for that. I tripped over his foot. He didn't push me. And yes, I'm certain—because I was behind him."

Apparently satisfied, though I wasn't, Sheila moved on,

Tripped over his foot? Did he put his foot in her path? Or had her path trespassed on his foot?

It mattered.

Eventually Sanders had his turn with her. I've worked with Sanders on a few occasions, which was why his note taking this time seemed odd to me. It wasn't his usual way.

Sanders was damned good at his job, and seemed to care about right and wrong, as well as winning. Of course, winning still came first.

"Just to clarify, Ms. Hamilton, was James Todd ever purposely violent with you?"

That professional smile came again. An odd time to smile, I thought. I wished I had even half a sheet from the tablet of paper Sanders was scribbling all over. Notes. I needed notes. But a spy with notes would be kind of obvious.

I waited for the answer, wondering if anyone would notice if I switched my cell phone to record. And immediately discounted that idea, too. They might not, depending on how discreet I was, but it would certainly be unethical and probably illegal without the classy lady's consent.

"Purposely? No."

"Would you classify him as a docile man?"

"He had a temper. He got angry." Ms. Hamilton's tone was unchanged from when she'd answered the birthday questions.

"With you?"

"When I did something stupid, yes."

Whoa. Hold everything. This paragon of correctness, this example of perfection, had just degraded herself. Probably not a big deal, but it seemed out of character.

And at the top of my personal list of symptoms of abuse victims compiled from years of professional experience—*victims accept the blame for the abuse.*

"Did you ever think he was capable of killing you? Or anyone?"

"No."

"Thank you."

I waited for Sheila to turn to me to ask if I had any questions. She didn't do so. Our little party was over. Damn.

DID HE EVER HURT YOU, physically?

Eyes closed, Jane laid her head back against the first-class seat late Friday afternoon, trying to lose herself in the muted sound of the engine, in the clouds outside her window. She'd have liked to have lost herself in the glass of wine the flight attendant had offered, but she didn't drink on planes.

She promised herself a glass when she got home, instead. While Pet ate, she'd sit with her. The bird would be extra clingy tonight.

Did he ever hurt you, physically?

She'd expected the question, of course, but still hadn't been prepared. Had he? Sure. On purpose? No. She had a Victim Witness file to attest to that fact.

The distinction was critical when a man's life was at stake.

Unless he was guilty and she was helping to set him free to hurt someone else. What did she really know about James Todd? How sure could she be that her judgment where he was concerned was trustworthy?

The flight attendant walked down the first-class aisle and back, checking to make sure everyone was comfortable. Jane felt her concerned glance land on her and wanted to run and hide. The day had taken more out of her than she'd thought. Drawing on years of practice, Jane breathed deeply, concentrating on relaxing the tightness in her body, one muscle at a time. And prayed to God that she'd given the attorneys the right answers.

"YOU'RE EARLY. I didn't have to circle." Brad saw her before she spotted his BMW in the throng of pickups at the curb outside O'Hare's baggage claim. Taking the handle on her roller bag, he tossed it in the trunk.

Feeling awkward, needing a hug that wouldn't have been forthcoming even in their good days, Jane climbed into the car.

"How'd it go?" Brad maneuvered them out of the curb traffic with ease.

"Okay."

Jane wasn't up to the crazy dance that being with Brad now required. She was too worn-out to marshal her defenses and keep him out. She should have insisted that Walt Overmeyer's man pick her up, rather than just waiting at her house, ready for night vigil.

She was tired of that, too. Of being constantly watched. Of feeling like she couldn't just take care of herself.

"You want to talk about it?"

"Not really."

That should do it. They could get through the rest of the drive in a silence that they pretended was friendly and say goodbye without any more awkward moments.

"I wish you would."

"What?"

"Talk to me about what happened in Ohio."

"Why?"

"Because I know you've had a hard day and I care."

Truth was a funny thing. It hurt like hell sometimes, and had the power to fill chasms in an instant. Brad cared. So did she. At the moment, caring seemed like enough.

"The deposition wasn't bad." Jane thought about the day, the couple of hours she'd spent walking around the town.

The Chandler courthouse took up a full block in the center of town—and served an entire county. Chicago had many court facilities—including one in Allenville—but none as architecturally impressive as the one-hundred-year-old Ford County courthouse. She hoped to God she never saw the inside of the place.

She told Brad about the prosecutor's office across the street from the courthouse. "I was only there an hour," she said. "And there were only the two attorneys and the psychologist who's an expert on the case. I'm not sure why she was there. I've already met with her. But Sheila Grant asked if I minded her sitting in and I didn't. Dr. Chapman never said a word. Overall, the day could have been much worse."

She stopped there. Meant to lay her head back and rest. "It's just that…"

Rest, Jane. Just rest.

"Just what?"

Glancing at Brad, Jane didn't want to think about

why she was doing this—holding herself apart from what she needed. He was a friend, nothing more. And nothing less.

The warm familiarity of Brad's strong profile, those dark eyes that compelled her to trust him, pulled her into a space she'd vacated. Their space.

"I'm struggling," she confessed. "I'm worried about my answers to their questions."

"Did you tell the truth?" He used the soft tone she'd never heard him use with anyone but her.

"Of course."

"That's all you need in a situation like this."

"And you know as well as I do that attorneys will take my words and spin them in whichever way works best for them. Be it defense, or prosecution."

They'd had this discussion many times before. He'd know she wasn't complaining, that she understood that every side had to be heard in order for justice to work.

This also wasn't the first time she'd given a deposition. She'd been asked, more than once, to testify at the request of domestic abuse victims at Durango. Usually when a defense attorney for the husband tried to belittle his wife's character or her fitness as a parent. Jane had been called as a character witness then, too.

"That's never bothered you before."

Not much, anyway.

"I've never been more than an informant before. They're acting like I'm a star witness here, and I'm not."

This was his game far more than hers.

"Rightly or wrongly, I feel like they're looking to me to make or break this case. What I say could send James to prison for life."

"What about his third wife, Marla?"

"From the little I've heard, she's going to be a hostile witness for the prosecution, if they call her at all. For all I know, she and James are legally married by now and the prosecution *can't* call her."

"The testimony of an ex-wife would hardly be enough to convict a man of murder, unless she happened to witness the crime."

"But if they can prove that the defendant showed a pattern of brutality to his wives, that could make the other circumstantial evidence much more compelling."

"So you think they're trying to get you to help them show that pattern of brutality?"

"Yeah. It was clear from their questions today." Their turnoff was eleven miles away. Jane wanted to just keep on going, off into the sunset with Brad.

"I get that it's hard, honey, but still, all you have to do, all you *can* do, is tell the truth. Don't elaborate. Answer the questions they ask and nothing more. That way you aren't steering either of them in any particular direction."

"But the questions they asked were so leading, I could hardly answer them with the truth without steering them. That's the problem."

"They're just doing their jobs."

"I know. I'm not blaming them, but it's not my job to decide a man's fate and I feel like I'm being forced to do so."

"I'd think the only pertinent fact here would be pretty straightforward. James didn't abuse you physically."

"Right."

Something in her tone must have alerted Brad to her unease. His sideways glance was quick and sharp.

"Did he?"

"No."

"Then that's what you tell them."

"I did."

He glanced her way again, his expression filled with concern.

"Are you sure you aren't just feeling a bit guilty testifying against a man you used to be married to?"

There didn't seem to be any personal edge to the question—a different version of Dr. Chapman's loyalty question. And again, Jane gave it full consideration—not all that difficult considering she'd spent the morning reliving many of the memories she had of those years.

"I really don't think so," she said slowly. "I don't feel any loyalty to James. The man betrayed me. He's a cheat and a liar—a bigamist. But that doesn't make him a murderer. I feel nothing but contempt for him. All the same, I don't want to help send him to prison if he didn't kill Lee Anne. And I don't believe that the man I knew was capable of killing anyone."

"Did you tell them that?"

"Yes. But the rest of their questions could be answered in so many different ways. I'm just not sure how they'll choose to construe my answers."

And what if she was wrong, and James did kill Lee Anne? What if he hurt another woman because something Jane said let him go free?

She'd tried to be responsible—to paint a true picture—but wasn't convinced she had.

"As long as you told the truth as you see it, there's nothing else you can do, Jane," Brad said. "In the end, a witness can only give one point of view. One perspective. The jury will hear many facts and the attorneys will do all they can to make both sides clear. If one construes your words one way, you can pretty much depend on the other to do the opposite. It's up to the jury to decide whose account is most accurate."

She was counting on that. Counting on individuals on the outside to extract the truth from a marriage she still didn't understand.

Brad's phone rang. He glanced at the screen and didn't take the call. Jane figured that Christine Ryan's name had popped up.

CHAPTER ELEVEN

BRAD OFFERED to buy Jane dinner. Or to take her to his place and make dinner for her. He even offered to have soup and sandwiches with her and Pet at her place if that's what she preferred. But Jane turned down all his suggestions, saying her stomach was a bit off and she wasn't going to eat.

He pulled into her driveway, noticing the nondescript sedan parked across the street, and waved at the man sitting behind the wheel. Jane had given the security company a description of him and his car, and made sure they had his license plate number, too.

"I miss you," he said, parking the car but not getting out.

"Don't, Brad, please. Don't put us through any more what-ifs."

"What if I think we're worth it?"

"The aftermath of what happened between us hurt me too much. Can you swear to me that you'll never hurt me like that again? Can you guarantee that we'll never make that mistake again? Can you honestly tell me that you don't look at me differently now that we've had sex?"

Of course not. He knew better and so did she. He didn't speak.

The expression on her face mirrored one from Emily's sweet face. One that haunted his nightmares. Back then, he hadn't known what to do about it. Now he did. He gave up. Because the pain behind that look was something he was never, ever going to cause again.

The knock on Jane's window had him throwing himself across her body before he'd even known he'd moved. It was the man from the unmarked sedan. Walt's man. Brad recognized the uniform and backed off while Jane rolled down the window.

"I'm sorry to bother you, ma'am, but I'm supposed to let you know that a package arrived for you at work today. Your assistant turned it over to Detective Thomas, who said that it contained a white powdery substance. They sent it for testing, but wanted you to be aware. We should check your mailbox here, to make certain that it's clean. And then we're recommending that you stay home from work tomorrow, at least until the results come back from the lab."

This time the look on Jane's face wasn't because of Brad, but he didn't hate it any less.

"I'm staying here tonight," he said. "I don't want you in there alone."

"No." Jane's voice was strong. "You are not. I will not be terrorized out of my home. Out of my life." Her voice might be a little shaky, but the determined glint in her eyes was not.

She allowed both men to go through her mail. After they found nothing suspicious, she unlocked her front door, waited while the security officer checked every room, and then locked herself inside. Alone.

But she didn't want to be alone. Brad was sure of that much. And was waiting for her call later that evening when his cell rang.

"What's up?" he said, answering on the first ring.

"Brad?"

"Jane?" He glanced at the screen. Yes, it was her. But he'd never heard that tone in her voice before. Fear? Shock? He couldn't place it, but his heart was pounding as he reached for his keys and headed for the door of his office. "What's wrong?"

"I… Are you…busy?"

Are you with Christine? he translated impatiently. Life was too damned complicated.

"I'm at the office going over some briefs," he said. He preferred work to anything that would give him time to think about Jane. He slid his Bluetooth in place and clicked it on. "I'm just leaving."

"Can you come over?"

"I'm already on my way."

"Okay." She didn't hang up.

"Brad?"

"Yeah?" The BMW slid smoothly out of the parking lot.

"This isn't… I mean, I don't want you to think I'm… It's not about… I… We just need to talk."

"I understand. Did something happen?"

"I… We can talk about it when you get here."

His insides dropped. Something *had* happened. He'd kill anyone who laid a hand on her. He'd…

Brad got control of himself. Jane had protection. A police force on alert. Even so, if he hit a red light he'd run it and explain later. "Are you hurt, babe?"

"Hurt?" Her laugh bordered on hysteria.

"Physically hurt. Did someone hurt you?"

She kept laughing and now Brad was just plain terrified. "Babe, Jane, listen to me. Do you need to get to the hospital? Have they called an ambulance?"

Please tell me you weren't beat up. Or worse.

"What?" The bizarre chuckles stopped. "Oh, no. I'm here alone," she said. "Except for Pet and my keeper outside. Have been all evening."

"Pet's okay, then?" That would have been his next question. She cared so much about that bird.

"Yeah. Except she's been screaming all night."

Which she only did when Jane was upset.

"Did you eat?" He sailed through another green light. Two more and he'd be there.

"No."

She didn't seem inclined to hang up and Brad scrambled for things to talk about, while his heart raced to her ahead of him.

She'd been in bad shape when he'd picked her up at the airport and the news about the package must have done her in. Whatever the reason, she was worse off than he'd ever seen her. Otherwise she'd never have called him. That was for sure.

"You should probably eat." It was dark. Which meant it was after seven. He glanced at the digital clock in his dash. Nearly eight o'clock.

"Probably."

"I haven't eaten, either," he said, though at the moment, food wasn't the priority it usually was. "We can make an omelet. I saw some ham chunks in the freezer the other night when I was there feeding Pet."

"Okay."

She sounded calmer. That was good.

"You sure you can't tell me what's wrong?" He was less than a minute away.

"I'm sure."

"But you're all right?"

"I don't know," she said, scaring him all over again. "We'll talk when you get here."

"I'm here." Clicking off his phone, Brad waved again to the man whose name he hadn't bothered to catch earlier, and put the car in Park.

Brad's phone rang again and the screen lit up with Christine's name. Leaving the cell unanswered on the passenger seat, he locked the car and let himself in Jane's back door.

HE LOOKED THE SAME TO HER. The irrational thought alerted Jane to her distracted state of mind. Of course he looked the same. He *was* the same.

Just as she was. She was the same woman who'd arisen that morning in a rented room in a bed-and-breakfast in Ohio and walked to the drugstore to make a purchase that she hadn't allowed herself to think about until she was safely home.

"Jane!"

She looked over at him from her seat on the couch. "Yes?" He was still wearing the navy suit he'd had on at the airport. Funny. She'd showered. Twice. And then she'd put on…what?

Jane glanced down at her favorite white silk ribbed pajama pants and top. They were designer and the softest things she'd ever owned. Satisfied that she was presentable, she watched Brad take a seat on the couch next to her.

"Babe, I've been talking to you and you aren't saying anything. You're scaring me, here."

That was understandable. She was scared, too. There. She'd finally admitted it.

"Talk to me."

She would, if she could figure out what to say first. What not to say. What was proper to say in a situation like this.

"I'm in shock." She started with the first fact that came to her. She needed her best friend but no longer had one.

"Just tell me what happened." He looked around the room as though trying to find some sign of why she was upset. "Has someone been here?"

"No. Just me and Pet."

"Did someone call, then?"

"No."

"An e-mail? Another threat?"

"No. No more messages. And the white substance was athlete's foot powder. I called Thomas. He'd walked down and picked up the results himself. He said that the threat was very clear, though. This guy means business, just not yet. I've still got time to do what's right." She giggled and could hear her own hysteria.

Brad touched her cheek. That hand. On her again.

She needed him. And he was too close. She couldn't let him get any closer.

"You don't feel warm to me. Did you get sick?"

"Yes." That was what had started it all. The nausea. After this morning's bout, she'd taken herself to the drugstore just to deny the fear before it took root.

"For the third time in a week. I'm pregnant, Brad."

And as she said the words, she suddenly felt calmer, as though her world had stopped spinning.

"Pregnant?" He stared right back at her. "How long have you known? How pregnant?"

"Completely pregnant. I took the test when I got home tonight. There were two strips in the box so I did both." And with those words the real truth struck and Jane, competent, self-assured Jane, who held back tears at all costs, started to cry in earnest. Thick wet tears, streaming down her face. There didn't seem to be anything she could do to stem the flow.

PREGNANT. Jane was pregnant.

And she was crying. Stunned, Brad had no idea what to do, except pull her into his arms and hold her while her body convulsed with sobs. He'd only seen Jane cry, really cry, once in the two years he'd known her. The day a client from Durango had been beaten to death by the husband she'd returned home to.

Pregnant. She was pregnant.

But...

Brad started to sweat, knowing that his worst nightmare had been nothing compared to this.

He'd wanted to spare Jane pain? Well, he'd done a fine a job of that.

And what about him? He couldn't be a father. Hell, he couldn't even be a decent boyfriend.

"IT'LL BE OKAY." Brad couldn't believe he was saying the plebian words at a time like this. How on earth did he know if anything would be okay? And yet, as he continued to hold Jane, as he rubbed her back and smoothed her hair away from her damp cheeks, they were the only words that came to him. Over and over again.

He wished he believed them.

She would be okay. He'd make sure of that. Somehow.

But him? Brad didn't have the slightest idea how to view himself as a parent.

The possibility had never crossed his mind.

SHE'D FALLEN ASLEEP. Hard to believe that, with all of the questions screaming for answers, she could just drop off, but Brad didn't begrudge Jane her rest. Rather, he envied her ability to find a place of peace. Lord knew she'd had a rough day. A rough month.

She said she hadn't eaten. He'd suggested an omelet, but maybe one of her favorite cinnamon crunch bagels would be better. As soon as she woke, he'd toast one for her. Or maybe, considering the nausea, plain would be better.

Certainly his next order of business would be to find some books. Books had answers. For her. He was thinking of Jane. Only Jane. This was about her.

Ironic that his goal that day in the woods had been to secure the possibility of love in Jane's future. To open her up to a romantic relationship with someone who would give her a great life.

He wondered how much having a baby in tow was going to harm her chances. And the thought led to another, one he'd ordered himself not to consider. What about him? Just the night before he and Christine had talked about the possibility of more than just professional interest between them. She knew he wasn't looking for a commitment. And had assured him that she wasn't, either. He wondered how she'd feel about hauling a baby on a date to the theater. Did people even take babies to the theater? He tried to remember if he'd ever seen one there. He didn't pay a whole lot of attention to babies. They belonged to other people. Until now. He'd have to take care of this one part of the time. It was the only right thing to do. Assuming Jane was going to have it.

As though reading his thoughts through her dreams, Jane stirred. Lifting her head from his chest, she pushed back to a sitting position. "I am so sorry," she said, brushing the hair away from her face.

She looked lost and alone and Brad wanted to pick her up and carry her to bed, to cradle her until morning. And stopped short. Where had that thought come from? He'd never been to bed with Jane. He'd made a baby with her, but had never once lain beside her in a bed.

"Are you hungry?" he asked, focusing on what he could actually do.

"A little."

"When was the last time you ate?"

"Breakfast."

"I'm no expert, but I'm certain that's not healthy. Anything sound good?"

When was it appropriate to ask if she planned to have the baby?

"Nothing."

"How about tolerable?"

Her shrug wasn't much help.

"How about a bagel?"

"Okay. But plain, okay? With a little butter?"

She got up to follow him to the kitchen. "I can do this," she said, reaching beyond him for the butter and knife as he loaded a bagel in the toaster. And because he didn't want to push her, Brad stepped back and let her butter her own bread.

"I SWEAR TO YOU, I didn't mean for this to happen." Brad sat with Jane while she ate. She'd covered Pet's cage before he'd arrived, probably to protect the bird from any emotional turmoil, but Brad still expected to hear from the sensitive creature any second now. Surely that thin piece of cloth wouldn't be enough to block their tension.

"I know that." Jane tore off a piece of bagel and slowly ate it.

"So…" He sat upright, watching her. "Are you, I mean, I assume you're planning to have it?"

"You know how I feel about abortion."

He nodded. He had his answer.

CHAPTER TWELVE

"JANE, WILL YOU MARRY ME?"

Jane, standing at the sink rinsing her empty bagel plate, looked over at the man leaning against the counter behind her.

"You're kidding, right? Though I have to say, the joke was in very poor taste. If I didn't understand that you're as much in shock as I am, I'd throw you out."

Brad straightened as she turned. "We're having a baby, Jane. And before that, we were best friends. Which means we have a lot more going for us than most people who get married."

She'd never actually seen someone look green until right then.

"You no more want to marry me than spend your life cleaning toilets."

Jane's throat tightened. She saw again those little strips in her bathroom. And then the static came, starting in her head and moving to her stomach.

She wasn't herself. Wasn't ever going to be herself again. She was in her house, but everything had changed. Everything was different.

Swaying, Jane caught herself with one hand on the edge of the counter. And slowly moved to a chair at the table in the windowed breakfast nook looking out over a rock pond she couldn't see in the dark.

"Brad, I can't marry you." One thing was quite clear—she didn't have any emotional stamina to spare. Some things just had to be dealt with and dropped. She folded her hands in her lap, meeting his gaze because it was the right thing to do.

"I can't marry you," she said again, more slowly, more kindly this time. "Look at us, we're barely even speaking anymore. You're seeing another woman. We're awkward around each other. And you want us to become husband and wife just because a stick turned a certain color? Because that's the only thing that's changed since you picked me up at the airport today."

But they'd been more than strangers in the car on the ride home. They'd at least been friends again for a few minutes.

"A child is far more than a stick color, Jane." Brad's tone wasn't as kind or understanding as it had been since his arrival. "You know that as well as I do. And of course things have changed. Now that we know about the baby, everything has changed. Nothing will ever be the same again for either of us."

His words, so close to her thoughts, sparked another bout of panic.

"But we aren't in love with each other. I've got trust issues and you make no secret of your aversion to commitment. We might make things easier for now—and that's a big might—but we'd only be borrowing from the future to pay for the present."

"This is no longer just about us. We have a child, another human being, to consider."

Shock reverberated through her again at his words. Her mind knew the facts but she couldn't seem to absorb them.

"A child is no reason to marry." She was sure of

that. "Much better to have two loving parents that have always lived separately, than to have to experience the confusion, guilt and pain of separation and divorce."

She only had to look at her own life to know that. Her parents' odd arrangement might not have been traditional, but she'd always felt loved and supported. She'd grown up happy, unlike a couple of her close friends who'd been dragged through their parents' bitter divorce battles.

Brad took her hands. "Look, Jane, I care about you. A lot. You know that. And you care about me, too, or at least you used to. We're having a baby together. Life isn't all clean and orderly. I got you pregnant and I'm going to do the right thing."

"The right thing isn't necessarily marriage." The idea was plain frightening. She couldn't even think about it. Marry Brad? A man who couldn't settle with one woman if his life depended on it? No way. Uh-uh. Never.

He sat back. "You plan to have the baby on your own?"

Sighing, Jane stood, peeked under the cover on Pet's cage and turned. "I don't know what my plans are right now, Brad. I just know that getting married just because I'm pregnant is a really bad idea. What about Christine? Are you going to tell me there isn't something starting between the two of you?" *And all of the other Christines in the future?*

His pause was enough. She couldn't marry him when there was another woman on the horizon. Been there, done that and was still paying for it.

"You'll have to stay home from work now for sure," Brad said next, wearing her out with his mental acrobatics. "The threats. With a baby to consider…"

The threats. She'd forgotten about them. Had actually forgotten that she was being stalked.

Thank God for the sink behind her.

BRAD DROVE HOME, then, after a quick change of clothes, jogged back to Jane's house just a few miles from his in the quiet suburb. He didn't try to see or speak to her. He was just running and had to go somewhere.

Lights shone through her front blinds. She was in there. Pregnant.

He stopped beside the sedan with Mr. He-didn't-know-who inside who now had two people to guard.

The man rolled down the window. Brad read the thin silver name badge above his pocket before speaking.

"Mr. Samuels, I'm—"

"Brad Manchester. I know." He rattled off Brad's license plate number.

Brad was impressed, feeling a little better, if that was possible.

"She's upset tonight. Keep a close watch, okay?"

"Always do."

"And will you call me if there's any trouble?" If he sounded like he was begging, it was a small price to pay.

"That way, is it?" the man summed up. "Okay, yeah, I'll call you if she so much as gets up to go to the bathroom during the night."

The guard was Brad's kind of man. And he had to be satisfied with that.

CHAPTER THIRTEEN

"WHAT WE HAVE HERE, Ms. Hamilton, is what we don't like to see—a perp whose threats are escalating and whose identity we don't know."

The brown-suited man in Jane's office spoke like someone on a TV police drama. But his grim expression wasn't make-believe. Nor were his credentials. Will Thomas had been a special detective with the Chicago police force since Jane had been in diapers.

Time's closing in. Do the right thing or the powder will do more than scare you.

Exchanging glances with Marge, Jane deliberately didn't look at Brad, who'd come running the second that she'd called this morning, the last Wednesday in April, informing him of the latest message and the resulting immediate police interrogation.

She'd thought, as the father of her baby, he should be kept informed.

Jane was still coming in to work, though she'd capitulated and agreed to allow herself to be driven by a bodyguard. And to have one outside her office door, as well. If someone was going to get her, he could do it at home just as easily as at work.

Every member of the *Twenty-Something* staff had been reinterviewed that morning. And officers were questioning all other employees in the building at that moment.

"We need you to think again," Detective Thomas said, glancing between the three professionally dressed people sitting on the couch in Jane's office. "Harder. This guy is certain that Ms. Hamilton knows what he expects her to do. If we don't find him, we better at least figure out what he wants."

"Other than Shawn Maplewood, I can't think of anyone. Or anything." Brad's voice was soft but authoritative from beside her. Jane tried her best not to lean toward him, not to need him at all. The only thing she had to fear was fear itself. She read the sign above her door.

The gray-haired detective made a note and looked to Jane.

"The only person I know specifically who has reason to be upset with me is my ex-husband. I've been called to testify against him in a murder trial."

She heard Marge's intake of breath but didn't look at her.

The detective swore eloquently. "Why didn't you tell me this before?"

"Because the threats started before any of this stuff with James. And I don't have anything to say that would hurt him. He knows that."

"You've spoken with him, then?" Thomas asked.

"Not in the five years since our divorce, but his attorney was at my deposition. He knows my testimony isn't going to hurt James. If anything, it will help him."

Detective Thomas handed her a notepad and a pen. "Write down his information. I'll check him out anyway."

Marge, her expression pinched and serious, named a couple of editorials that had garnered negative attention from some of their readers. But this was nothing new; she'd already turned over all of the letters to the police.

Brad shifted, his thigh touching hers. It had to be an accident, but she was grateful for it all the same.

They talked about families again. Neighbors. Former employees. All things they'd already gone over.

"And no ex-boyfriends?" Detective Thomas asked again.

"No," she said immediately.

"I can't stress enough that you shouldn't go anywhere alone," Thomas said. "Not out to water your plants. Not to the grocery store."

Jane listened, feeling like some kind of freak sitting there in the midst of them.

"You're scaring me," she told him.

"Good. In a case like this fear could keep you safe." Thomas stood.

"Detective, in your experience, how often do threats like these end in violence?" Brad asked, facing the older man.

"It's possible that this is a hoax, a way to scare her, to make her squirm, with no intended danger to follow. Most people who stoop to anonymous notes are cowards. But my personal hunch is that this guy's serious. Either way, we can't take any chances."

Jane swallowed past the lump in her throat and silently shook the detective's outstretched hand.

As soon as Brad was alone with Jane in her office, he faced her.

"I'm moving in with you." Maybe a little stark, but he got his point across.

"No, Brad, you aren't." Jane's smile was filled with

compassion. For him? She was the one who needed protecting.

"You're pregnant, Jane. And in danger. You can't stay there by yourself."

"Oh, yes, I can."

Earlier her hands had been shaking. Now she seemed completely self-possessed.

"This is serious, Jane."

"You think I don't know that? I feel someone breathing down my neck every waking moment. I can't even sit in a room anymore without making certain that my back's against the wall."

Good, so she got it. "Then you realize that you aren't safe on your own."

"I'm as safe on my own as I am anywhere, at the moment," she said, sipping from a can of diet cola. She'd told him that now that she was pregnant, she was allowing herself only one a day. "I've already called for extra locks on my windows and doors and I'm upgrading my security system to include motion sensors around the house."

The tension in Brad's shoulders increased.

"What I'm not going to do is run scared. I'm not going to let some coward control me or my life. This could go on for months. Years. And there's a chance it might never develop into anything. Whoever is doing this is not going to rob me of my life."

He recognized the Durango rhetoric.

"You aren't in a safe house, Jane."

"If I give in to fear, I might as well be in prison. I won't take unnecessary risks, but I'm not going to let this creep make me a victim, either."

Seeing the set of her shoulders, the resolute look in

her eye, Brad knew he was fighting a losing battle. For now.

"You're carrying my child." He still couldn't get that to sink in. He was going to be a father. He had no idea what that meant, practically speaking.

"I know."

"We're going to have to talk about that."

"I know. But not now. I have a lot of work to do."

"When, then?"

"Saturday? Sometime after my appointment?" She'd called him when she'd made the OB/GYN appointment because she'd agreed, that first night, to keep him in the loop. And had avoided any further reference to the baby until now.

"I'll drive you in."

"No. That's okay. I have a couple of things to take care of here afterward. But we could talk later when I get back. We could meet at your office."

"Fine, but I'll meet you at the doctor appointment, as well."

Brad considered it a major victory that she didn't argue, though he had no idea what he'd just won. He had no idea what he wanted from Jane or for himself.

He just knew that he shared responsibility for the mess she was in and, as such, had to support and look out for her. Whatever that meant. Whatever it cost him.

JANE DIDN'T WANT to think about nurseries, cribs or child safety locks. She didn't want to look at baby name books. She didn't want to be pregnant. She didn't want to have trained professionals guarding her house, escorting her to work and standing around waiting when she went to the bathroom.

And she did not want to be called back to Chandler, Ohio.

But not wanting something didn't make it go away. She couldn't change the circumstances, but she could choose how she dealt with them. She could choose whether or not they made her a victim.

And so, in spite of shuddering every time she thought about the newest threat and her meeting with Detective Thomas two days before, she went about her business as normally as she could the rest of Friday. Worked in the car as she was driven home, and spent the evening reading over the initiatives her marketing team had presented in a meeting that afternoon. Every light in the house was on. She sat at the dining room table with her back to the wall, with a full view of both the living room and kitchen. Her mace and cell phone were close at hand, and a kitchen knife was planted under an open folder.

She planned to work until thoughts of turning off the lights and going upstairs alone didn't fill her with terror. Eventually, she gave up and went to bed anyway.

The next morning, riding to her obstetrician appointment in the backseat of the car her boss, Barbara Manley, had, as of the day before, assigned to her, Jane wasn't thinking about possible assailants. Or demands. She wished that her mother wasn't off at sea. Jane had tried to call a couple of times but reception was sketchy at best and she hadn't been able to get through. Her mother had been through this—single and pregnant and knowing that marriage would be the wrong choice. She'd probably have some reassuring words.

Not that Jane and her mother had ever confided

in each other much. Theirs was more the "how's the weather" type of relationship.

Saturday mornings were supposed to be enjoyable, not eaten up by doctor's forms and waiting rooms.

As they reached the Chicago city limits, Jane's entire body tensed. She looked right and left, watching every move on the street. And knew that whoever was sending her threats was succeeding. She was terrorized. It had to stop.

Forcing her mind onto other topics didn't help much. She was pregnant and on her way to learn what the next months of her life would hold. She was responsible for the beginning of an entirely new life that she hadn't planned or wanted.

Her stepbrother and his wife, who, at twenty-seven, already had three offspring, would think it was about time she started a family. Though, with their strong religious beliefs, they'd probably frown at the idea of her doing so alone.

Still, they'd be a source of advice when Jane actually had to do something besides try to keep food down.

Or she could just do an issue on first-time motherhood. With her talented staff, she'd have all the best advice and information at her fingertips in a matter of weeks.

Having a partner to share the overwhelming burden of decision-making would be nice, too.

Jane spotted Brad's black BMW parked in front of the doctor's office and leaned forward to ask her driver to pull over.

Where Chicago's downtown streets were normally buzzing, on Saturdays they were lazy.

Just as Jane wished she could be.

"Hi. I was getting worried." Brad met her as she got out of the car.

In casual slacks and a polo shirt, his presence was reassuring. More than reassuring. Her first instinct was to take his arm and lean against him as they crossed the sidewalk.

"I didn't want to be early."

Falling into step beside her, he held the door to the building open. "How are you feeling this morning?"

"Fine."

Physically. Which was a blessing. She was on her way to a highly personal and private examination with him beside her. And had no idea what he was to her, what he could be to her. Ex-best friend, one-night stand, father of her child.

"I have to be in Chandler again on Monday. They want me to speak with Dr. Chapman one more time."

Sheila Grant had called that morning and left Jane feeling very uneasy. The prosecutor seemed intent on believing that Jane was hiding something. It seemed to Jane that the woman was desperate to get a win at any cost. Even possibly sending an innocent man to jail for life.

"Why would the psychologist want to speak with you again?"

"More like Sheila wants me to speak with her. Something to do with the deposition. It sounds as though they're going to want my testimony after all."

"You didn't have to agree to the meeting."

"I know. She made that clear, but I have nothing to hide. And I don't want to live with the responsibility of having either put an innocent man away or allowing a guilty one back on the streets, unless I know I've done all I can to be impartially fair."

"No one expects you to be impartial, Jane. You were married to the man and he betrayed you. It's okay to hate him for that—and to let the jury see the pain he caused you."

"What he did to me has absolutely nothing to do with a woman falling off a cliff."

"It could if it shows that the man is capable of being emotionally cruel."

Emotionally cruel. Odd that Brad had used those words, ones that she might have used to describe James herself. Once or twice. Not as a general rule. But still...

After checking the directory by the elevator, Brad pushed the up button. "Are you flying out that morning?"

"No, Sunday night. My appointment's first thing on Monday. I hope to catch a three o'clock flight back."

"You have a safe place to stay?"

"Yes."

"I'd like to take you the airport." It seemed to be the one part of their relationship they couldn't give up. As though, as long as no one else took Jane to and from the airport, they were still them.

"Fine." Was his conscientiousness just because of the threats? Or the baby?

He'd called her every night since they'd found out she was pregnant. Each night she'd told him she was fine and asked him about his case with Christine. Without giving her specifics, he'd told her that he was pleased with their work so far.

Jane had listened, then thanked him for calling. She'd

refused to engage in personal conversation with him, which she knew wasn't fair. But she needed time to assimilate.

By the look on Brad's face, her time had run out.

BRAD JOGGED after returning home from the doctor Saturday morning. Jane was working and they'd arranged to meet later that afternoon to discuss the baby. After five miles, he circled back to his place and spent the next hour lifting weights. He called around to see if he could find a game of basketball but everyone in his extensive circle had plans.

He couldn't call Christine, even though he knew she was free.

Their case was coming together and as for something more personal…how did he sleep with one woman when he'd just gotten another pregnant?

He was going to be a father. Jane was six weeks along and the doctor said everything looked good. Their baby was due on Christmas Day.

He couldn't run fast enough to outdistance the fear. And he had no idea where his life was headed. He'd bear the financial responsibilities without a second thought. Any more than that rested on the mother of his child. That point had come home very clearly to him that morning. He'd not been invited into the exam room. This was Jane's body. Her journey.

He would have rights after the baby was born, he knew, sitting in the empty waiting room filled with women's magazines and toddler toys. If he wanted to assert his rights as the baby's father—meaning, if he wanted legal obligation to pay child support and get visitation rights—he could take Jane to court, though the thought of them being on opposite sides of a courtroom was ludicrous.

He ran the vacuum and cleaned the master bathroom. He never used the second bathroom down the hall.

Christine had been making it obvious she was interested in a more personal relationship. She was a beautiful woman and ordinarily he'd have been completely occupied by her.

He hadn't yet told her he was going to be a father. He didn't know what to tell her. How much of a role he was going to be playing in his child's life? What kind of a father would he be if Jane wanted him to take an active role? He helped women maintain custody of their kids. He rarely actually interacted with the kids themselves.

It wasn't that he had anything against kids. They were a necessary part of the process of life. Just not an intimate part of his life.

How had life become so convoluted? So twisted?

Eventually, after exhausting all the other avenues of time expenditure that occurred to him, Brad showered and went to the office. Jane wouldn't arrive for another couple of hours, but he had a pile of briefs that were more than willing to occupy his Saturday. And his Sunday, too, no doubt.

Now that he no longer had a best friend to go hiking with.

An hour into a three-hundred-page divorce file he'd inherited from an attorney facing a bar complaint that would probably cost him his license, Brad heard the bell downstairs. He answered it in record time.

"Are you okay?" he said, pulling Jane quickly inside and watching as her driver parked and turned off the car.

"I'm fine, Brad. Quit fretting so much. You're going to make me a nervous wreck and that's not good for the baby."

"Have you eaten?"

Seemed like all he did these days was worry about this woman's stomach. Aside from worrying about her safety, that was.

She shook her head.

"Anything sound good?"

"You won't believe this."

"What?"

"Pizza. Pizza sounds great." When Jane grinned, the glimpse of his old friend was a kick in the gut. He missed her more than he'd ever have thought possible.

"You don't like pizza."

"I know. But a ham and cheese pizza with onions and tomatoes sounds heavenly."

"Then let's order one."

"Now?" The shadows were back.

"Why not?"

With a shrug she followed him upstairs.

"YOU SEEM DIFFERENT." Brad sat on one end of the leather sofa in his office. Jane was on the other—an open box of half-finished pizza on the coffee table in front of them. "More at peace."

Maybe. While she stayed in this place that was familiar and yet was outside her normal life.

"I'm on shaky ground," she told him. "Six weeks ago I was on top of the world. Life was exactly what I wanted it to be, where I wanted it to be. I had a full schedule, people I care about. A best friend..."

"And then it all just came tumbling down." She was rambling, but he seemed to be content to let her do so.

And talking was better than going quietly crazy on the inside.

"Maybe you're getting a wake-up call."

"Yeah, well, I'm willing to wake up from this nightmare. Who's calling?"

"You're the only one who can figure that out. It's your life. But you've definitely been shaken up a bit. Maybe you were too complacent, letting life pass you by."

"What about you? Life's kind of passing you by, too. Why didn't you get a call?"

Sitting forward to snag another piece of pizza, Brad gave her a wry grin. "Maybe I did. Maybe that's what this baby is. I don't know," he said. "Tell you what, if I figure it out first, I'll give you the answer. If you do, you do the same, huh?"

She grinned back. "We're a piece of work, aren't we?"

"Which might or might not bode well for the child we're bringing into the world."

Yeah. They were doing that.

"I guess we need to talk about that," Jane said, her stomach in knots again. Brad was right. In some sense, she was more at peace. "I'm okay with it."

"With what?"

"The baby." Saying the word didn't strike the same chord of fear it used to. "It's strange, but seeing the doctor today, hearing her say that everything is fine, being treated as though this is all normal and I'm no different from any other woman, made it all real. I have a list of things to eat, vitamins to take and an exercise goal. I can handle this."

"Of course you can."

"It's like I had to hear her confirm that I was pregnant before it became a reality."

"Facing something tends to make it easier to handle."

Jane stared at him, sensing a deeper meaning, but unable to put her finger on it.

"I would've liked to have been in the room with you," he said, "hearing everything firsthand."

"I didn't want you there."

"I gathered that. I'm just not sure why."

"Because I… It was too personal."

Brad frowned. "It's not like I'd have been standing at the end of the table watching, or like I haven't already seen it all," he said dryly and Jane heated up.

She had a deal with herself that she wasn't going to think about the way she got herself into this position to begin with. She'd banned herself from thinking about Brad's hands—and other things—now or in the future. Thinking about it all turned her into an insecure woman she didn't much like and certainly wasn't willing to live with. Having him see her in any state of undress right now…too personal, just like she'd told him.

Still, he was her baby's father. There were going to be some intimacies.

"Well, anyway, I realized something this afternoon."

"What's that?" His gaze was relaxed, as though he'd be okay no matter what she thought or did.

"I want this baby. I wouldn't have chosen now to get pregnant, and certainly not the way I did, but I'm going to love this child—I already do. I'm kind of excited, now that I'm getting used to the idea. Nervous, but excited."

"Seriously?"

"Yeah." She smiled up at him. "Weird, huh?"

He looked her straight in the eye. "Maybe not."

While her pizza should be revisiting her by now, it

apparently had other ideas. Jane felt better than she had in weeks.

"We need to talk about practicalities."

She'd known this was coming. "Okay."

And they did. Brad insisted that he be a part of the process. Now that she'd accepted the situation, Jane could see that it was only fair that he be as involved as he wanted to be. Just because the baby was using her body for its incubator didn't make it any less his.

When she let herself think about it, she had to admit the truth. "I want you to be a part of our baby's life," she said. "You're the father. Children need their fathers as much as they need their mothers."

What it all meant in terms of their own relationship she had no idea. But Brad took his responsibilities seriously. If she denied him this, he wouldn't be able to live with himself. She cared about that. And about him.

"I don't know how to work things—I haven't even thought about it yet—but you'll need to start thinking about a room, baby stuff, a car seat."

His lips tightened, but not in anger. The expression was new to her but it only took a second for Jane to realize that the man was scared to death.

"I have to do the same," she added quickly. "Maybe we could shop together sometime. Get car seats, all that kind of stuff. Figure it all out."

"That'd be great. Thank you."

Jane nodded, wondering if this would ever stop feeling surreal.

So they'd do it together. A team.

"But I still can't have you around during the…medical parts," she insisted after another minute of thought. "That would just be too…odd."

"What about when the baby's born? Will I be there then?"

How could she know? That was months and months away. And there was so much to do before then. She had to deal with threats, a trial and redesigning her life.

"Do you want to be?"

"I think so."

Definitely the blind leading the blind. Jane felt like a lost kid, wandering around, but having no idea what to look for. Or how she'd know when she found it.

"Let's revisit that when we get closer to the time."

Brad seemed satisfied with that.

"So we're friends again?" he asked.

She studied him, sitting back on the couch, meeting her gaze, and didn't know what to say.

"I can't go that far." She gave him all she could. "I... Things have changed between us, Brad. You're not just someone I hang out with anymore. In one sense, I've got a higher stake in your decisions. The things you do, the choices you make, will ultimately affect my child. I'm not going to be as nonjudgmental. You know?"

He watched her, still saying nothing.

"The women you're with, they'll come in contact with my child."

"You don't approve of my lifestyle?"

This was why she didn't want to have this conversation. At least partly. "I'm not saying that." Or maybe she was. "It's just all so...convoluted and messy now."

Jane cared in ways she'd never cared before. She hated the fact that he touched other women as he'd touched her. Which made very little sense to her since she was sure she didn't want a sexual relationship with him.

Brad liked women too much for her comfort. She'd shared a husband once. She never would again.

And since she wasn't confident that she'd be able to tell when her husband had another woman—or wife—on the side, she had to pay close attention to character traits and avoid certain ones. Like womanizing.

Not that she and Brad were in love. Or would ever seriously consider marriage.

"I… You proved your point, Brad. I'm sexually alive. I'm not the asexual friend I used to be."

"Your sexual feelings, they're for me?"

"I do not want to have sex with you." There was no doubt about that.

"That's not what I asked."

"Once I'm in a position to start dating again, to spend time with other men, these feelings will spread to them."

Brad was the only man other than James to have ever made love to her. Of course he was the object of certain…feelings.

Certain that he was going to press her, she was surprised when he suddenly sat forward and closed the pizza box.

"So we'll be a team, for the baby's sake, and leave the rest to the future," he said.

"Okay."

"With one stipulation."

Jane stood, ready to refuse. This was one situation she could control. At the moment, she was the one in possession of the child.

"I'd like you to keep me apprised of your whereabouts at all times. With the threats, and you being pregnant and alone—"

She cut him off. "Fine."

She had to get out of there before she did something crazy. Like ask the father of her child to have sex with her again. No strings attached.

CHAPTER FOURTEEN

Monday, May 3, 2010
Chandler, Ohio

I SKATED BY MYSELF first thing that morning. Deb, my receptionist and sometime skate buddy, likes to snuggle with her hubby in the early mornings. I've got Camelia, but there's only so much snuggling one can do with a four-pound toy poodle.

I skated ten miles, though I'd have liked to have done twenty. It was going to be that kind of day.

Sometimes, when I'm called as an expert witness, I meet with the client once, give my opinion, and go on my way. Sometimes I don't even meet with the client—I just declare what I know to be true about a particular malady and my job is over, when, for instance, someone has already been diagnosed. And sometimes, like with the James Todd bigamy murder case, I'm asked to take a more active role.

Almost always when Sheila was involved.

Last week, I finally met with wife number three, Marla Anderson Todd, who had now officially become a wife and claimed the right to refuse to testify against her husband. After three missed appointments, it had taken a court order to get her to keep an appointment with me. A court order based on the premise that James could have manipulated Marla into marrying him. I wish

I could have gotten to her before her second marriage ceremony solidified, in her mind, that she believed in her husband—that she could prove her love by being loyal to him.

She'd agreed to meet with me again, though. Whether she'd keep the appointment remained to be seen.

"Tell me about James Todd," I said later that morning, facing wife number one, the calm, cool and collected Ms. Hamilton. A woman who, by the way, wasn't under court order to see me, but who'd agreed to do so anyway.

"I have nothing more to add than what I've already told you." Jane Hamilton sat perfectly straight in the armchair across from mine. The same one she'd chosen before.

I waited.

Her long dark hair was twisted into a sleek knot, almost as though it was glued in place—no stray tendrils falling anywhere. Certainly not on the shoulders of the obviously expensive silk suit she wore. Eyeliner, mascara, blush—all perfect. Did the woman have a crew assisting her ablutions every morning?

I had to resist the urge to blow the bangs off my forehead. I usually love my messy, Meg Ryan–type hairdo. Mostly because it means I can shower, blow-dry and go. And I'm blonde so I figure I can pull it off. Most of the time. Right then, looking a little more sophisticated might have been nice.

"I want to help in any way I can," Ms. Hamilton continued in a polite, but also sincere, tone. "I simply don't see what more I can do."

Everything about this woman was perfect, which told me that something was very wrong.

"Tell me about you, when you were married to him."

"I was freelancing for magazines by then. I'd just graduated from college, which is where I met James. He was one of my English professors. He was also the one who set me up with my first contacts. As a matter of fact, the article that catapulted me to the bigger times was his idea. It was a piece on athletes who'd been offered substantial scholarships to play college ball but had turned them down. As one who'd turned down a football scholarship, he offered to be interviewed for the article."

I was more interested in the fact that she'd married her college professor. A person who had built-in authority over her.

"Why didn't he take the scholarship?"

"His dad was sick and needed care."

"Where was his mother?"

"She ran out on them when James was two. Left them for a man with a lot more money than a factory worker would ever make."

"So James's father worked in a factory?"

"Yes."

"He was an only child, then?"

"No. He had an older sister, but she went to live with her mother when she was in high school."

"But James did go to college." He had to have.

"Yes. He got an academic scholarship at a university close to home so he could care for his dad. He has his doctorate in English."

"Do you think he resented losing his chance to play professional sports?"

"No more than any other guy would have. He was a defensive lineman and always said that the chances of a debilitating injury were greater than the chances of making a living in football. He was glad to have something reliable to fall back on."

Ms. Hamilton sounded like any other wife talking about a man she'd loved.

"What does James do now?" I could ask Sheila, but the information wasn't pertinent to the case. Only to the woman in front of me. Or rather, her answer might be pertinent.

"I have no idea. Last I knew he was teaching at Wright State."

"So he made good money."

"Sure."

"More than you?"

"At first, of course. But not toward the end of the marriage."

"And you? You said you were freelancing. Did you work from home?"

"For the first couple of years, yes. Then I got an offer to edit in New York...." She named a magazine everyone who could read and had been at the checkout of an American grocery store would have heard of. "I still did a lot from home, but commuted back and forth to New York once or twice a week."

"So you were away from home a lot?"

"Only during the day. I always flew home at night."

"Must have made for some long days."

"I thought it was worth it."

"Worth it. How?" I caught myself about to chew on the end of my pen and pulled it away from my mouth.

"Worth it to save my marriage. Worth it to be able to have a career I loved."

"So your marriage was in danger after only a couple of years?"

"No!" It was the first real emotion I'd heard from the woman. Interesting. "I mean, no," she said more calmly. "But James and I agreed that a healthy marriage took work—and two people together at the end of the day."

But the man had had two wives, hadn't he?

"So he was home every night, as well."

"For the first few years. He'd spearheaded a master's program involving New England Literature studies and he traveled with students to tour homes and study collections."

"So his career came before the marriage."

I knew I was poking her.

"No. He hadn't planned to teach the class himself, but I encouraged him to do so. The traveling was only going to be a few times a year once he got the curriculum set. And he was due to be promoted to department head, which was what he'd always wanted."

"So you didn't mind him traveling?"

"I understood that it wasn't forever."

"Did you miss him when he was gone?"

"I was busy, but, yes. I was used to him being there."

"Did you start spending more nights in New York?"

"On occasion, if I was working late, but not usually. We had an elderly Sheltie who was a rescue pet. We had a sitter for her, but I didn't like to leave her too long."

"Who rescued the dog? You or James?"

"James heard about her. We went together to get her."

And Jane took on the mother role—being at home to tend to the child.

"What happened to the dog?"

"She died of old age about a year before we divorced."

"Back to the traveling. Did you resent the fact that he
could leave you alone at night for his job, but you were
killing yourself commuting home from New York for
yours?"

"Of course not. I made choices."

I liked Jane Hamilton. I'd never seen anyone try so
hard to be honest with herself. And I worried about her,
too. No one was as together as she seemed to think she
was—at least not that I'd seen.

I had to remind myself that she wasn't my client. By
my own rules, I wasn't to get involved on this one. Or
to care beyond human decency.

I had a job to do and little time in which to do it. And
Ms. Hamilton had some mighty impressive barriers for
me to get through. I had best get busy.

BRAD WANTED to take Jane out to dinner when she
got home Monday night. He'd been up late the night
before reading pamphlets the doctor had given them and
wanted to talk to her about possible tests during pregnancy. Most of which he hoped she'd opt out of unless
something unforeseen came up that would specifically
require them. According to the doctor, some were entirely optional. They seemed pretty risky for minimal
practical gain. But still, he and Jane should discuss them,
though the decision would ultimately be hers.

Jane was tired when she landed. Pleasant to him, but
tired. She said her meeting with the expert witness had
been uneventful. At her request, Brad dropped her off
at home for a solo dinner of toast and cereal to be followed, she said, by a hot bath and an early night. She'd

promised to read the materials he brought and call him in the next day or so.

Nice and platonic and…professional.

And that, after a full day at the office and in court, left him with another vacant evening to fill with exercise. He was going to be the fittest lawyer in Illinois before this year was through.

There were only so many baby books a guy could get through without scaring himself to the point of sleeplessness.

It wasn't as though he could admit his fear to anyone—even himself most of the time. He was a guy and not at all used to being vulnerable.

In his basement, beating himself at a game of billiards, practicing for a local charity tournament later in the summer, Brad dove for the phone when it rang. Maybe Jane couldn't sleep or wasn't feeling well.

Maybe the guard outside her house was calling.

Maybe she'd been thinking about him and wanted to be touched again…

Where that thought came from Brad had no idea. And quieted the instant reaction of his body with a huge pang of guilt. For getting Jane pregnant. For Emily. For continuing to have sexual feelings for his best friend.

The caller wasn't Jane.

"Christine, how are you?" he said when he saw her name on the caller ID.

"Good. I just came from the Advocacy Networking dinner," she said, naming a Chicago organization that promoted professional relations between lawyers and the Illinois judicator. "Bill Wilson was there."

A well-known Illinois defense attorney. Brad had played hoops against him during an Illinois law school alma mater face-off a few years ago.

"He once defended Shawn Maplewood."

Adrenaline pumping—healthy adrenaline—Brad switched gears, becoming all lawyer.

"Defended him? I thought Maplewood didn't have any priors."

"Not under that name he doesn't. But he wasn't Shawn Maplewood then, either. He goes by his mother's maiden name these days. Bill called me back with a case number, which I've just looked up."

"What were the charges?"

"Domestic abuse against his live-in girlfriend and her four-year-old son."

"Did he do jail time?"

"A year."

"We need to rewrite that brief and get it to the judge and Shawn's attorney, asap. How soon can we get together on this?"

"What are you doing tonight?"

"Driving to the city, it sounds like."

"We could meet at Julian's." A quiet pub halfway between Allenville and Chicago where they'd met before. "Or," she continued, "you could come to my place."

He had a baby on the way.

"Julian's is fine. Meet you there in half an hour?"

"I'll be waiting.…"

He wondered how he was going to respond to the invitation he'd heard in her voice when they were face-to-face. How should he?

Maybe, for Jane's sake, he should take care of his sexual needs before they created another problem between them.

But only if Christine knew the score.

THE REST OF Jane's week was consumed with watching every shadow, trying to force food into a permanently knotted stomach and putting the Intimacy in a Technological World issue to bed. A lack of communication between Marketing and Editorial made for a tense afternoon as tempers flared over space that had been claimed twice.

One of her freelancers had gotten herself into trouble in London—nothing to do with the magazine, thank goodness, but her story on fall fashions for the twenty-somethings was going to be too late for the July issue and would have to be replaced—making it the second time that particular journalist had let her down.

It was also the last. Jane sent an internal memo to that effect.

She'd also heard that James's trial would start the following Monday. She was going to be called as a witness for the prosecution—though the exact date and time would depend on how quickly they got through jury selection and opening arguments.

The good news was, there had been no further threats.

Detective Thomas warned her not to let her guard down. He said that her stalker might have lost interest, but it was more likely that he was getting ready to strike.

Jane hoped the guy was just an attention-seeker. But considering the fifty-something detective's record and his low-key demeanor, she didn't think so.

He'd had an Ohio police officer do some checking on James Todd and the man hadn't left the state since his original arrest. Nor had his wife. He could hardly have mailed threats from Chicago himself. The officer had questioned James about the letters without disclosing the content. James denied sending anything to Jane, claiming that he didn't even know her address.

"Sheila Grant wants me in Chandler Tuesday afternoon," she told Brad Saturday morning as she traipsed just in front of him up a slight incline in a walking path not far from their homes. He'd called and invited her to hike an easy trail—and because she was tired of her treadmill regime already, and couldn't very well exercise outside alone until her stalker was caught, she'd jumped at the chance.

She tried not to look behind her every step of the way. Tried to ignore the fact that a professional watchdog followed close behind them.

"How are you doing with the idea of testifying?"

"Great." The trail widened, allowing them to walk side by side again. "Okay," she amended. And then said, "I don't know. Uneasy, I guess."

"You'll be seeing James."

"Yeah, and of course that has me on edge. How could it not? I haven't seen him since our divorce—and certainly not since finding out the extent of his betrayal."

"With you being a witness for the prosecution, he can't talk to you or even come near you."

"I know. And to be honest, it's going to feel good to be away from Chicago for a day or two. Away from threats and stalkers and bodyguards."

"Have you told Detective Thomas you're going?"

"Yeah. He likes it when I'm out of town." She stepped over a clump of weeds. "Sheila Grant will be providing any transportation I might need. And I have a room in a B and B right by the courthouse."

Brad frowned, but didn't say more. She wondered if he knew how badly she needed freedom from all the stress. Some sense that she could take care of herself.

"I keep having this dream," she continued. And who

else was there to tell except the man next to her? The only person she'd ever really confided in.

"I'm on the witness stand but I'm outside it, too, watching myself there. I always start out dressed in a suit—the colors change, but they're all suits. And then suddenly I'm in white shorts and they're too short. I feel self-conscious about them. And I've got on this pink-and-white-striped top. I hear myself talk, and I know I'm lying. That I'm perjuring myself. I can't understand what I'm saying, but I can't make myself shut up, either. Then suddenly I'm out in this dusty yard and surrounded by men wearing chaps and cowboy boots. James is there, dressed in a dark suit with a red tie and shiny wing-tipped shoes. He's up on a scaffold with a rope around his neck and no one can see me but him. I'm supposed to save him, but I don't. I just stand there."

"In your shorts?"

"No. I'm back in a suit. It's getting dusty. That's all I remember."

"What's the significance of the shorts and top? Do you recognize them?"

"Nope. They're nothing I've ever owned or would even wear. Come on, Brad, can you see me in pink stripes?"

"With your dark hair, pink would be good on you."

His compliment meant far more to her than it should.

"Sounds to me like you're still taking too much responsibility for something that you aren't accountable for at all." Brad grabbed her hand to help her over a small ditch.

Because she was pregnant, she was sure. Jane tried not to feel anything, not to acknowledge the wave of pleasure that swept through her at the touch of his hands.

What was wrong with her? She'd never had a hand thing before.

But then, she'd never had reckless sex on a hill before. Or been pregnant before, either.

She'd never had a best friend with whom she'd had sex.

"Whatever happens to James Todd is because of him," Brad continued as though unaware of how the earth had just shifted for her. "The man's made some pretty poor choices in his life and now they're catching up to him. If the jury sees a man capable of murdering his wife, it will be because of the picture painted by the life he's led."

"Sheila told me that his third wife, this Marla Anderson woman, married him again a couple of weeks ago, legally this time. She's now claiming spousal privilege and refusing to testify."

"And you can rest assured that Todd's attorney will make certain the jury hears that she was willing to marry him in spite of the charges. Implying that she believes in him, that she knows he's innocent, because what woman would marry a man who'd murdered his wife?"

Surely that information would influence the jury more strongly than anything Jane might say about him.

So why was Sheila Grant so convinced that Jane's testimony was necessary?

WITH BLUE SKIES and seventy-degree temperatures, this was a perfect May Saturday. Jane wondered if Brad had been with Christine the night before, if they were sleeping together.

And cursed the random thought—an echo of the others that occupied her otherwise rational mind at inappropriate moments throughout her days and nights.

"Sheila Grant has already heard what you have to say and she thinks your testimony is valuable or she wouldn't be calling on you." Brad's warm voice pulled her back to the conversation at hand. "All you have to do is repeat what you told her and you'll do fine."

"That was different. I wasn't being examined and cross-examined, I just told what I know."

"And that's all you have to do this time."

She was sure he was right, but still couldn't shake the restlessness that grew worse whenever she thought about James Todd and the Ohio court case.

Or imagined Brad and the beautiful attorney, heads bent close, as they perused some dusty old law tome.

She was on her own. Everyone, the prosecutor, Kelly Chapman, James's attorney, the judge, the jurors, even James and Marla Anderson Todd—they all had their own jobs to do, their own lives and issues separate and apart from her.

As did Brad. And Christine Ryan.

The whole thing left Jane—sad.

CHAPTER FIFTEEN

"DID YOU READ THE STUFF I gave you?" Brad walked beside Jane, keeping his hands in his pockets. Didn't matter how beautiful she looked in her formfitting jeans and loose white top that matched her tennis shoes. Or that the dark tendrils falling out of the clipped knot on top of her head gave her an air of fragility.

What mattered was that he was having these thoughts. That he was noticing something like a "tendril" in regards to his buddy.

"About the tests?" she asked, frowning as she stepped over some roots. "Yeah. I read it."

"And?"

"I'll schedule a first trimester ultrasound like Dr. Williams suggested."

"Agreed."

"I don't want to consider any other tests unless she thinks I need them for the baby's or my health."

"Agreed again."

"Do you want to know the sex, if they can tell?"

"Not really. How about you?"

"Nope. They don't know for sure, anyway, and I don't want to expect one thing and get another."

That didn't sound like his Jane—who preferred controlling her environment to being surprised.

No, not his Jane. Definitely not his. She was the mother of his unborn child, but her own woman.

They discussed possible dates and times for the first ultrasound during the month of June.

"I'll want to be in there," Brad said, hoping she wouldn't argue with him. The more he saw, the more he knew, the better prepared he'd be for whatever lay ahead. "I want to see what the technician sees, to hear what he has to say." He'd read about the exam, knew the kinds of things that could be either discovered or ruled out.

"I know."

"In the room."

"I know."

"I've already set up a trust fund for the baby, and a separate college fund," he rambled, getting everything out at once before she could start saying no. "And my name should be on the birth certificate." That way Jane and their baby would be protected if anything happened to him. And would be certain to have financial support until the child turned eighteen, as well.

Brad knew the law.

"And I'd also like to establish formal visitation rights. Not that we have to adhere to them if we both agree, but just in case, you know, you get married or want to move out of state, or..."

God, he sounded like a divorce attorney. Felt as though he was listening in on one of his own consultations, only this time he wasn't just the attorney, he was the client.

And he'd seen firsthand how heated things could get between two people who'd vowed to love each other forever.

He hadn't chosen to become a father. He *wouldn't* have chosen it, but with this baby on the way, he had to think about its needs and about his obligations. One thing was for certain, he didn't want his child growing up thinking he didn't want him or her. Or care.

"Of course." Jane didn't miss a beat.

That was it? No argument? But then he and Jane weren't ending a relationship. They weren't enemies fighting for what was left in the ashes of bitterness and disappointment. He and Jane were friends. Who happened to be having a baby.

"WANT TO REST?" Brad stopped at a fallen tree. The stream they'd been following branched around into an inlet, but they wouldn't be going there. The area was far too secluded.

Jane wasn't the least bit tired. But she agreed anyway, sitting on the tree to face the stream as she pulled a bottle of water from the small pack around her waist. She took a sip, savoring the cool trickle down her throat, and, without thinking, offered the bottle to the man who'd sat beside her.

Walt Overmeyer was off to her left, watching her.

Jane hated the reminder that there was likely someone out there who was willing to hurt her to get his way.

But when Brad accepted her bottle and took a sip after her, all thoughts of her stalker fled as a rush of longing swept through her body. Hard to believe it had only been seven weeks since the last time she and Brad had hiked. He'd asked her to open up to him. And he'd made her pregnant.

"I miss you," she said.

His elbows on his knees, Brad clasped his hands, tapping his thumbs together, almost as though he had no idea what to do with them.

"We were good together," she continued when her brain told her to shut up.

He nodded.

"Hard to believe anything could have changed that."

"I know," he agreed with a quick glance in her direction.

"Are you still seeing Christine?" Why she was obsessing over the woman, Jane didn't know and didn't want to know. She just wanted to get over it.

"We've been working a lot."

She watched the stream run over rocks, the landscape constantly changing yet staying reassuringly the same.

She had a baby on the way now. Another life to consider—a child who would need her at her best. She couldn't afford to lie to anyone—most particularly herself.

"She's not your usual type."

"I wasn't aware I had a type."

True. Brad wasn't partial to either blondes or brunettes, judging by the women she'd seen him with. Tall or short didn't seem to matter, either.

"Your women are usually more jaded. And dedicated first and foremost to themselves and their own pleasure."

He didn't say anything.

"Christine's different," Jane persisted, irrationally piqued by his silence. "Is she the one do you think?"

"Which one?"

"The one you're certain you can love for eternity? The one who inspires you to take the risk at commitment." Because Jane obviously wasn't. There, she'd admitted it.

Admitted, too, to herself, that she was scared to death that Christine could be.

He glanced her way again. "Does it matter?"

"If she's going to be around my child it does."

Brad didn't look away, but Jane couldn't decipher the message in his intent brown eyes. "I'll let you know if and when that's an issue," he said.

Jane wondered if she'd offended him. Angered him.

"I…didn't just want to know because of the baby," she confessed. "I…care about you, Brad. You're my friend. I want you happy."

"Thank you." He nodded, then stood. "You ready to move on?"

As ready as she was going to be. Jane joined him on the path and hoped that moving on didn't mean moving further away from Brad.

He didn't touch her again the rest of the afternoon. Jane hated that she noticed.

HOW COULD TWO PEOPLE CARE about each other so much and yet be so uncomfortable around each other? The question plagued Brad as he drove into the city later Saturday for a night at the theater with Christine Ryan.

He still had no answers as he pulled up in front of Christine's elegant home. They were going to dinner first, at a bistro downtown that catered to the legal circle.

Jane had asked if Christine was the one. His immediate answer had been no. Irrevocably no. And how could he have been so certain?

He was just getting to know the woman. And so far, he liked everything about her. He was attracted to her.

How could he be so certain that he wouldn't fall in love with her?

As a man people turned to for answers, he seemed to have surprisingly few for himself.

Tired of his one-man show, Brad immersed himself in the cacophony of lawyers ridding themselves of the week's tension over dinner, and then tried to enjoy the production of *Mamma Mia*.

And because he was so determined to get out of his head, Brad, for the first time since he'd met Christine, didn't think about business once while he was with her.

He did think about Jane.

"I'D LIKE TO TURN my third bedroom into a nursery," Jane chattered as Brad drove her into O'Hare airport Tuesday morning for her flight to Ohio. "Two yellow walls, two green, with a yellow-and-green-checked border."

If she thought about the baby, she was fine. She could stay calm and in control.

After more than two weeks of silence, she almost wished her anonymous stalker would send another message. Let them catch him so she could get on with her life.

"Green's my favorite color."

"I know. Yellow's mine."

"I remember."

"And bears," she blurted. Lots of teddy bears. All sizes. "I'd like to have a trunk with bears sitting on top of it."

"Sounds nice."

"And I need a comfortable rocker. I did some looking around this weekend and I found this sleigh glider that I really like. In cherry with foam-green upholstery." She pulled a picture she'd printed off the Internet from the front of her briefcase and handed it to him.

Glancing at it as he drove, Brad said, "Nice."

She'd been thinking all weekend about what would happen after the baby's birth. Just how much of a role was Brad expecting to play? As in hours in a day. And days in a week. Brad didn't seem like the stay-at-home father type. But then, in the time she'd known him, what did he have to stay at home with? Or for?

He certainly was good with kids. At least from what she'd seen at the shelter. And he'd taken a personal interest in Jason Maplewood.

They had to talk about visitation and their expectations, but not now. Not today. Today she wanted to think about yellow and green and gliding.

And about the work that was going to be her distraction over the next several hours as she waited her turn to speak at court. There'd be a private room where she could wait at the courthouse. Or Sheila could phone her at the bed-and-breakfast down the street where she'd be staying.

The prosecutor had called early that morning to confirm that she'd arranged an escort for Jane from her room to the courthouse. Court security had also been alerted.

Today, Jane was going to be seeing James Todd again for the first time since she'd divorced him. Today, she couldn't afford to think about Brad's days or where he spent them.

BRAD WAS IN HIS OFFICE, preparing for his last meeting of the day, an out-of-town client whose divorce trial was scheduled for the next morning, when he saw Jane's number flash on his cell.

"How'd it go?"

"I had a bout of morning sickness on the stand almost as soon as I sat down and had to leave. They had other witnesses scheduled for the rest of the day. I'm going back tomorrow."

Though she had a flight booked the next afternoon, he knew she'd hoped to be home tonight. He'd purposely scheduled his working dinner with Christine late, so he'd have time to get to the airport if Jane made it in.

"That's a lousy break. I'm sorry, sweetie."

"Me, too. When Sheila told me I'd be going on today, I gave up my room at the bed-and-breakfast. It was already taken by the time I made it back there."

"Where are you?"

"At an economy motel out by the highway. It's the only place within thirty miles of here. There's a truck stop on one side with a fast-food counter, and a family diner on the other. Nothing else but farmland."

A far cry from the Chicago suburb she was used to, or the bustling city where she normally spent her days.

"Does anyone know you're there?"

"Yes. The prosecutor dropped me off herself. She said she'd already spoken with the chief of police and they'll be doing extra patrols tonight. I guess it's standard for out-of-town witnesses. I'm really perfectly safe here. The place is filled with families and the adjoining restaurant is open all night."

"I still don't like the idea of you so far from town."

He knew he was overreacting.

"It's not like the stalker is going to be some random

trucker. He has no way of knowing that I'm in Ohio. Anyway, I have my mace. My cell phone's charged and I'll keep it by my side. My door is locked. And I'm tired. I'll probably go to bed early and work myself to sleep."

He still didn't like it. "Are you feeling better?"

"I feel fine." Her chuckle was dry and filled with weariness. "I picked up a chef salad for dinner and my stomach wishes I'd get off the phone and eat it."

Was that a brush-off? Brad wasn't ready to let her go yet. "Did you see James today?"

"Yes, though I didn't have anything to do with him. The only time I looked at him directly was when Sheila asked me to identify him."

"How'd he look?"

"The same, I guess."

"At ease?" A defendant's demeanor told stories.

"I was so busy fighting nausea, I hardly noticed him."

Her ex-husband had made her sick. Or the tension of having to see him again had. Or Brad's baby had.

"Did you see Marla?"

"No. Or, if I did, I didn't know it was her. I stayed at the bed-and-breakfast across the street from the court-house as Sheila had arranged. A deputy came to get me when they were ready for me."

"So you have no idea how the trial is going."

"Nope."

Odd that, now when the facts were finally being dis-closed, she didn't seem to want to know them—this from a woman who always had a million questions. He wanted to ask why. To find out what was really going on inside her. But every question that came to mind seemed to cross the boundaries they'd established. He was allowed access to her medical information and had input into every decision concerning their child. But her emotions—her deepest thoughts—were off-limits.

"I guess I better let you get to your dinner," Brad finally said. His client was waiting. He also had to prepare for his evening with Christine. They were going over an amendment Shawn's attorney had sent over in response to the new motion they'd written, agreeing to give up shared custodial rights if Kim would agree to visitation supervised by a court-appointed designee at Shawn's expense.

Christine did not want to accept the proposal.

"How was your day?" Jane asked in lieu of hanging up.

Was she finding it as hard as he was to let go?

"Good. Fine."

"What about the hearing? Wasn't today the Lido case?"

She'd remembered just like always, though, as usual, she didn't know specifics that weren't public record. "Yeah. It was tough, but the judge ruled that the best interests of the child negated the standard order of visitation."

Which meant that, in spite of the fact that there'd been no abuse or neglect, a seven-year-old girl didn't have to spend time alone with her alcoholic father. Hopefully he and Christine would be as lucky with Jason Maplewood.

"You won." Her tone had softened. "Congratulations."

His body reacted. And Brad knew a moment of pure panic. He was a damned Pavlovian dog, reacting to stimulus without desire or thought. He had to be. He'd just been worrying about Jane too much. Whatever this was wasn't personal.

It would pass.

CHAPTER SIXTEEN

Wednesday afternoon, May 12
Chandler, Ohio

MARLA ANDERSON TODD was late. Surprise, surprise.

Except this wasn't a meeting arranged by Sheila Grant. Marla had asked to see me.

I waited in my usual chair, notepad on my lap, trying to keep my mind clear for the third Mrs. Todd. I couldn't do my job if I already had a plate full of preconceptions.

But in this case, not having opinions was proving difficult.

One wife dead and two others swearing the man charged with the killing wasn't violent.

Five after six and no Marla. She'd asked me to meet her late because her husband, who was out on bail, had a men's club dinner that night. I wondered what the other men at the meeting thought of socializing with a suspected wife murderer. Surely they all knew.

Maybe they believed in his innocence. I'd seen the man that morning when I'd testified. He was certainly convincing sitting there so calmly, walking with his head held high, meeting gazes eye to eye. Maybe because he was innocent.

Six-ten. My sofa was still empty. It had been around for years, but its flowered chintz still looked inviting to me. But then I don't pay much attention to it, kind of like the baseboards and iron registers in the floors of the old building.

It was probably time to redo the whole office. I wasn't sure when I would have the chance to do that. As it was, I only had one evening at home this week. Camelia was going to be filing for divorce.

"Dr. Chapman?"

Marla Todd stood in the doorway. I'd told her to come on back when she arrived since Deb left at five.

"Yes, Marla, come in." I stood and ushered her in, closing the door behind her.

"Can this be off the record?" the blonde, athletic-looking young woman asked, standing with arms crossed just inside the door. She couldn't even be thirty yet.

"That depends on what you have to say. I'm working for Sheila Grant. However, if you tell me something that has no bearing on the case, then there is no reason for me to mention it."

"You're supposed to get me to admit that I've got some dark secret where James is concerned."

"No, I'm only supposed to try to help everyone find the truth. And to give an overview of the characteristics of manipulators and their victims."

"You think James is a manipulator? How can you know that when you've never even spoken to him?"

"I didn't say that." And I wasn't going to say it, either. Labels were handy for generalities, but specific cases were always more complex. "Would you like to have a seat?"

"No. I'm not staying."

My pad was on the arm of my chair. I wasn't going to increase Marla's mistrust of me by taking notes while

she spoke, but I tended to think better with paper nearby
and a pen or pencil in my hand. At least I had that. I'd
carried my pen over with me.

"So what can I do for you?"

"The last time I was here you said something about
my being certain I was speaking for myself and not for
James."

"That's right."

"You said that if James did kill Lee Anne, I could be
next."

"It's possible."

"I just want you to know that there is no doubt in
my mind that my husband is innocent. I went away last
weekend, with James's blessing, to a women's spa retreat
and I came back with a sense of utter peace. I am so
certain of this that I'm willing to stake my life on it. I'm
standing by my husband."

With James's blessing. My alarm bells rang. "Did
you speak with James at all while you were there?"

"Only when I called him. He wanted me to have this
time to myself to search my heart and know for sure that
he was telling me the truth. By the end of the weekend,
if I had any doubts, he would quietly go on his way."

Uh-huh.

Of course, it was possible the man really was a gem
who'd been falsely accused. Albeit a weak one who
couldn't make up his mind which woman he loved most,
or a selfish one who wanted a cookie in each hand.

"James knows he made a terrible mistake, marrying
two women at a time," Marla continued. "He's been
searching his entire life for a soul mate—the one person
he was meant to love. That was all he ever wanted. He
just got so caught up in his quest, he made the mistake

of rushing things. He kept two wives, two possible soul mates at the same time until Jane left him.

"And then he met me. And he knew he'd found what he'd spent his life searching for. The only problem was that Lee Anne wouldn't divorce him and he was afraid of losing me."

If I believed this, which I think I did, didn't Marla's explanation point even further to the possibility that James Todd, who'd already lost sight of the law in his "quest," would do anything to remain attached to that soul mate once he'd found her? Even if that meant murdering the opposition?

Not that my job was to determine a man's guilt or innocence. I was only here to observe the emotional and mental states of two women. And to help, if I could. That was always my personal goal, no matter who was paying me.

"Did James ever speak to you about Lee Anne?" I asked, willing to stand in my doorway for as long as this woman would stay.

"He told me about the marriage."

"Before he was arrested for her murder?"

"No." Marla's expression hardly changed. "But I understand that, Doctor," she said with more self-assurance than I've probably ever felt. "Think about it. What man would willingly push away what he valued most?"

"He didn't trust you to stay with him if he came clean?"

What kind of soul mate connection was that?

"He didn't want to hurt me. James is entirely focused on my happiness. That might be hard for someone like you to grasp, but I am a very lucky woman, Dr. Chapman. Most women I know would die to have a husband as loving and attentive as James is. When I'm with him, I feel like a princess. Like I can do anything. I know every minute of every day that I am loved and adored."

A rare piece of heaven? Or manipulation? James had effectively made a slave out of Marla Anderson Todd.

"You know, James tried to love those other two," she continued. "That's James. That's why I know he could never, ever hurt either one of them. James Todd is a lover—a tender, emotional being."

"How do you know how he was with his first two wives? Did he tell you?"

"I know because I know him. And because I heard him on the phone with Lee Anne once. I knew he'd been married and just assumed he was divorced."

My fingers itched to write. This was critical territory.

"And you remember what he said to her?"

"Every word," Marla said. "I was so impressed that he could be kind to her, even after all the hell she'd put him through, playing on his emotions, leading him on, threatening him…"

"How was he kind to her?" The woman was there to convince me that her husband was a good guy and I was stringing her along. I knew it. But if there was something unhealthy going on, I'd be helping her in the long run with any potential discoveries, any misrepresentation I might expose.

At least that's what I told myself. Maybe I was just doing the job I'd been hired to do.

"He told her that he had every right to come after her, and that if he did, she'd lose, but that, instead, he was going to give her everything she asked for."

"He was going to give in to her blackmail, you mean, rather than exposing her to the police."

"What blackmail? After the murder charge James

confided that they'd been talking about their divorce. She was demanding the house, all their possessions and all the money in their accounts. He told me that as far as he was concerned, she had it coming to her because it meant that he could give himself completely to me. That freedom was worth more to him than money and possessions. She'd given him a great gift."

I was listening, and getting the feeling that I was missing something vital. So I looked further. And then it occurred to me. He'd said he was going to give Lee Anne everything she'd asked for. That she had it coming to her...

"He said the same thing about that Hamilton bitch last night, too," Marla continued, her expression souring for the first time since she'd come into my office. "James made her what she is. He was her professor, did you know that? He's the one who taught her how to write a great article. He even got her several early pieces, including the one that turned into her big break. And how did she repay him? She took a fancy job in New York and had her own life. He thought he was building a life with her, and she'd only been using him. But he doesn't hold a grudge. He says she put him on the path to me. He's just so thankful to be here that he has only gratitude for her."

"If what you say is true, you'd think he'd at least feel some animosity. Remarkable that he has such a pure and forgiving heart. That doesn't happen often enough."

"I know. That's what I'm telling you, Dr. Chapman. My husband is an amazingly giving man."

"But he can't be that perfect, Marla." I felt compelled to try once more. "Sometimes, the appearance of perfection hides a multitude of sins."

"I'm not saying he's perfect," Marla quickly inserted.

"He believes that the Hamilton woman should pay for what she did to him, but he says the laws of fate and karma will take care of that. He says she'll get what she has coming to her."

Alarm bells rang so loudly I couldn't hear the woman standing before me. She'll get what she has coming to her. Lee Anne would get what she had coming to her...

James Todd wasn't going to let anything stand between him and Marla. He was going to protect her opinion of him, protect their relationship, at all cost. Or was it just that he was a man who made women pay to punish his own mother for deserting him?

And that was when I remembered the anonymous stalker that Sheila had told me about. The one who'd been threatening Jane Hamilton. Who was still in town.

By all accounts, James Todd was a man filled with evil, who did evil acts, but was also a genius at making those acts look like others had done them. Or made them look like accidents.

Like a suicide...

Making a hurried and probably rude excuse to Marla Anderson Todd, I ushered her out and ran for my phone.

A HOT BATH SOUNDED GOOD. Determining that the rather small tub was passably clean, Jane poured a bit of the travel-size bath gel she carried in her overnight bag beneath the faucet and watched while bubbles exploded under the streaming spray. She'd soak, relax, then climb into bed with her salad and the *Twenty-Something* proof she'd brought to review.

And maybe, unless she found a load of sense between

now and then, she'd call Brad. Just to reassure him that she was fine. He'd sounded worried. And she had to face it—one excuse was as good as another.

Still in her slacks and blouse, minus only the jacket she'd worn to court that morning, Jane thought she heard a knock on the door as she turned off the faucet. Straightening, she listened but didn't hear anything else. Her next-door neighbor must be having guests.

Feeling safer with people close by, she undid the top button of her pink blouse. Maybe she'd forgo the bath.

When the knock came a second time, her heart started to pound as she froze in fear. It was definitely coming from her door.

Who would be coming to see her there?

Then she remembered that the lady at the front desk was going to be bringing her the lost cord for the free Internet hookup she was supposed to have. This luxurious highway abode hadn't caught up to the wireless age yet.

At the door, she glanced through the peephole and saw nothing but blackness. What should have been glass was, instead, plugged rubber. Apparently luxuries didn't extend to working peepholes, either. The door wasn't visible through the window, and with the security dead bolt there was no chain.

Hearing voices outside as, she assumed, a family checked in close by, Jane thought about the clerk's double duty as room service and front desk representative and, knowing the woman was busy, opened the door.

And froze.

"Hi, baby. Long time no see, huh?" James's voice was just as she remembered it—soft and genteel. Sending no alarm signals to the family who got their bags into the room two down from hers and shut their door.

James's voice hadn't ever sent alarm signals to Jane, either.

Had it to Lee Anne?

"I saw Sheila Grant turn in here with you earlier," James continued easily, as though she cared. "I was on my way out to the club. I ordered a drink but couldn't find the patience for the small talk that went with it, and before I knew it, I was back in my car and coming here."

"You shouldn't be here." She was a witness for the prosecution. They'd told her he couldn't speak with her. He risked a mistrial and almost certain jail time while he awaited a new date.

Holding on to the door, she kept it mostly closed, standing in the opening.

He shrugged, the sheepish smile that had first tugged at her heart in class all those years ago appearing on his face. "I know. I thought about the damage I could be doing to my case, but in weighing that against the chance to see you, to make sure you're okay after what happened in court, well, what can I say? Here I am."

"And you have to go."

"I will. I don't want to cause a scene, I just had to see you. Knowing you were so close…I just kept thinking… remembering. You looked bad this morning, babe, like you were suffering. I'm afraid that my lapse of judgment, my infidelity to you, left lasting marks."

Marks like, say, the inability to trust that I'd know when a good man came along?

"I'm fine, James. Now go." Her phone was on the table just a couple of feet away. If she could get to it, she could call the police.

Or she could holler and someone in the parking lot would hear. There were several people out there, walking from their vehicles to the restaurant or motel office.

"Okay," he said, his glance warm and contrite at the same time. "You're one hell of a classy woman, Jane. I should've done better by you."

"What about Lee Anne?" she couldn't help asking, though she knew she should have just closed the door. But this was James, a man she'd lived with for more than five years. And her college professor before that. "What happened there, James? How'd you get yourself in this mess?"

Dumb, Jane. You know how. He was a bigamist creep. A charmer. And he charmed the wrong girl— one who fought back.

But that didn't mean he'd killed her.

He'd never abused Jane. She'd made certain of that. She'd educated herself and gotten the opinions of professionals. It was only the infidelity that had made her quietly walk away.

"I didn't do it, Jane, I swear to you," James said now, looking her straight in the eye. "I wasn't going to say anything to you about it. I know that's inappropriate and unfair and I wouldn't put you in that position. I'll never forgive myself for how much I've hurt you already."

Like Brad hated himself for hurting Emily? Was that it? James just hadn't loved her enough? The thought didn't ring true, but it made a strange logical sense.

"Believe me, if there was any way I could turn back the clock, I'd be the best damned husband you could've wanted. And I damned sure wouldn't have been unfaithful to you."

"I know Lee Anne was a student, too, James. What about your current wife, Marla? Did you teach her?"

His head dipping shyly, James said, "I have to admit, Marla was a student, of sorts. She wasn't in my class, like you and Lee Anne were—I wouldn't have been that gullible. She was part of that graduate study New England tour we were starting up those last couple of years you and I were married."

James was a leech who went after students. There was a pattern. Knowing was some relief.

"The program took off and we had applicants who weren't actually students, but professionals who wanted to take the class. Marla was one of those.

"But I didn't come here to talk about Marla. I came to apologize for what I did to you. Lee Anne...I made a mistake. You were traveling back and forth to New York. So high society all of a sudden." He glanced up at her, and she recognized the longing she read in his eyes. Longing for acceptance, for forgiveness and for love. It made her sick.

"You have to go."

"I know, I'm going, but...you asked, so let me tell you about Lee Anne. Let me tell you what really happened. I can't stand the thought of you thinking I'm a murderer."

"I don't think that."

"I know you must hate me for cheating on you, but I wouldn't have thought you'd be vindictive. That's just not my Jane. Which was why I was surprised to find out that you're testifying against me."

"And I'm not sure why they want me to. I've repeatedly told them that I don't think you'd kill anyone."

"Then help me, Jane," he said, his voice growing more compelling. "Please."

"James, I can't. You have to go."

"Let's at least talk about it," he said, glancing around. "Let me in, Jane. Let's talk."

She had a sudden glimpse of how this would look in Brad's eyes. James sweet-talking her, her capitulating—like so many abused women. Like a victim. Falling prey to the manipulations that had held her captive. She took a firmer hold on the door. "Go, James. Now." She pushed on the door, closing it in his face.

Except that it didn't close. His hand, quickly inserted between the door and the jamb, wouldn't let her lock him out.

"Back up, Jane," he said firmly, in a different voice. One she also recognized—his "I'm the teacher and I'm the boss" voice. "Please. I'm going to open this door."

Please. She hated that word. "I—"

Before Jane could say anything else, the door flew open with such force she was knocked backward. Her chin stung where the door struck her and her hand bent completely back to her wrist as she landed on the floor.

CHAPTER SEVENTEEN

6:36 p.m. Wednesday, May 12, 2010
Chandler, Ohio

"SHEILA, PICK UP. Now!"

Pacing in my office, I spoke into the prosecutor's home answering machine. I'd already tried her cell three times.

"Kelly? What's up?" Sheila sounded slightly breathless and I didn't even want to know what I'd interrupted.

"There might be trouble," I said, telling her what I feared about James Todd and Jane Hamilton, without telling her how I came to that conclusion. Now wasn't the time to figure out the ethics on that one. "I've already called 911, but I knew you'd want to know now in case this changes your strategy for court in the morning."

More than that, I was hoping the prosecutor would reciprocate. Tell me something. I was worried sick about Jane Hamilton. And the woman had barely given me the time of day.

"I should have called you." Sheila's reply surprised me. "Judge Summers ordered a mistrial. This afternoon, after court, Marla Anderson was seen talking with one of the jurors. Apparently their mothers used to know each other in art league."

Welcome to small-town justice. Even for a murder

trial, the jury pool was only so big, and no one had moved to have the venue moved to another county.

"So what happens next?" I asked, hating the bright colors in my chintz couch at the moment. I stuck a pencil in my mouth and spit it out when I bit too hard.

"A new trial date's been set for later this summer."

"And in the meantime?"

"What do you mean?"

"James Todd, what happens to him?"

"He's still out on bond. He probably doesn't even know. This all just happened. And I have no reason to ask the judge for a higher bond. The man's been a model citizen and has shown no signs of either skipping town or being a danger to society."

"Unless he's paid a visit to Jane." I had a feeling about this one, but hoped this was one of the times I was wrong.

"I'll give her a call," Sheila said. "But I doubt Todd would be stupid enough to go out there."

"Call me when you hear anything," I said and hung up.

For now, there was nothing more I could do. Except go home to Camelia. I was already very late for dinner and royalty didn't like to be disappointed.

"JANE!" That voice. He was still there.

Stunned, Jane picked herself up off the floor, aware that James was kneeling beside her, his expression filled with concern. "Oh my God, baby. I had no idea you were still standing there. I told you to move."

The door was shut now. And bolted. That's all she could focus on. That lock closing her in with him. But that made sense. James wanted time with her and James almost always got what he wanted.

"Jane, talk to me, baby. Should I call someone? Do you need an ambulance? I'd take you to the hospital myself, but you know I can't be seen with you. For both of our sakes. Oh, baby, your chin is swelling. I'm so sorry...."

Oh, baby, your foot is swelling. I told you to move out of the way....

"No," she said, still slightly dazed. "I'm fine."

I'm fine, James. Don't worry. You didn't hurt me.

She'd walked around with a broken foot to prove the point.

The memory triggered another. A faint and very distant memory of another tumble down the stairs. They'd been in his office at the university. James had been angry with her and she'd tried to get away from him. He'd attempted to stop her but hadn't wanted to raise his voice and draw attention to them. He'd followed her to the stairs. She'd pulled away with such force that she'd fallen down the stairs.

One of his students had seen the whole thing. The way James had tried to grab her, to save her. The way he'd broken her fall.

A terrible accident that had left her bruised, though otherwise okay, but had left her husband panicked.

His eyes. They had the same desperate look in them now. "Oh, God, Jane, this is terrible. I'll be sent to prison for sure now. And I didn't even do anything! But who's going to believe that? Look at you! I can't believe this happened. I can't believe you didn't move. I told you to move and..."

As his voice rose in panic, Jane came to her senses, just as she had so many times in the past.

"It's okay, James. Really. I'm fine. No one needs to

know." Her wrist might be sprained. Her chin stung, but her jaw was fine. And she didn't hurt anywhere else.

The side of the bed had broken her fall. Thank God. At least the baby…

Oh my God. He could have hurt the baby.

He can't know about my baby. That was her only thought now. Her only concern. She had to get rid of him.

"But they're going to ask you on the stand if I ever hurt you," James said.

Jane couldn't think about that. Couldn't think about anything but protecting her unborn child.

"It was on the list of questions Elliot showed me."

The baby. She had to keep James away from her baby.

"I've already told them you didn't ever deliberately hurt me, James," she said quickly.

Give him what he wants so he'll go.

"And if you go now, they won't even know you were here tonight," she assured him.

"What will you tell them about your chin?"

"I'll tell them the truth. I fell in my motel room. I was just getting ready to take a bath," she added, remembering the tub filled with water. "People slip on wet floors all the time."

"No!"

Stepping back, Jane put the bed between them. Between him and her baby. She'd forgotten how intimidating he got when he was agitated.

It had been that way in the classroom, too, which had garnered him a lot of attentive students who learned well. And earned him good teaching credentials as a result.

"Lee Anne was hurt in a tub once," he said now. "She really did slip. Don't mention the tub."

Lee Anne had had accidents during her marriage to James, too?

"Fine. I tripped on that tear in the carpet," she said, noticing one by the door. "My heel got caught and I hit my chin on the table."

"Don't say that." Jane had never been able to tell if it was irritation or derision in his tone when he got like this. "It's a lie. You'll just be opening up an opportunity for that Grant woman to prove that something isn't right. You're a terrible liar, Jane. Just tell them you lost your balance by the door and hit your chin on the wood. That's the truth."

How did he do that? Tell a lie within the truth.

"You were sick this morning. You probably had a bit of a dizzy spell because you're still not well. I didn't push the door hard at all," he said, his voice calming. "You hit your chin on the way down, I saw you."

That wasn't how Jane remembered it. But then, she was still feeling a bit thickheaded. She hadn't yet fainted because of the pregnancy, but she'd heard of plenty of women suffering from bouts of light-headedness. And she hadn't eaten and…

And if James had wanted to hurt her, he could have done a lot worse than a bruised chin, right? Just like he could have done more than dropped a weight on her foot. He could have hit her with it, slammed it into her face.

But what about the tennis match? The broken nose? What about the stairs at home? And the school ones? Oh, God. How could she have forgotten those stairs? How could her brain have betrayed her like that?

Still, none of that mattered. She had to keep her baby safe.

"I'm sure you're right," she told her ex-husband. "I haven't felt well all day. Just go, okay? Get out of here now while you still can."

"You're sure you're all right? I'll take you someplace if you need me to," he said. "I'm serious, Jane. The case aside, nothing is worth having you hurt…"

"No, I'm fine. Go." Once he was gone she'd be better. She just needed him gone, away from her baby.

Hers and Brad's.

"Okay." Hands up, James headed for the door. "I'm really sorry, baby. For everything," he said, taking hold of the knob.

"I know." *Go. Please. Go.*

"You forgive me? For the past, I mean. I didn't hurt you tonight, thank goodness."

"I forgive you." *Get out. Just get out. Get out.*

"And your testimony?"

"I'll tell the truth, James. Nothing's changed there."

"That I never deliberately hurt you?"

"Right."

"That the tennis thing, that was your fault."

"Right."

"Take care of yourself."

She planned to.

"You're a good woman, Jane. I know you'll do the right thing."

Do the right thing. The words that had been haunting her for weeks.

"You wrote those letters."

"I knew you'd listen to me. You always did. I have

an old student in Chicago who was happy to mail them for me."

Oh, God.

"There's nothing illegal about writing letters to an editor. Not when, in every single issue, you ask for readers to write to you."

So, in the end, he found a way to make the stalking her fault, too?

"Be happy, baby," James said now, at the door. "You'll always have a piece of my heart."

He paused, as though giving her a chance to respond, but Jane couldn't find the strength to do so. She just needed him gone.

"I understand, baby. And...thanks."

With a long, intimate look of longing, James slowly walked out the door. Confident as always that he was right. That he'd get his way.

"Come on..." Alone in her room, still shaking, trying to ignore the constant throbbing in her wrist, Jane begged out loud. "Please answer."

"Hi, you've reached Brad Manchester. Leave a message and I'll return your call as soon as I can."

When she heard his voice the tears started to fall.

"Brad? It's me. Please call." She hung up before she told him how much she needed him.

Dinner was at Christine's place. Brad had known, when he accepted the invitation, that he was treading dangerously close to the edge of a precipice he'd been determined to avoid. But they were due in court in a couple of days for the final Maplewood hearing and they had to be ready to defend any case law Shawn's attorney might use to try to persuade the judge. A little boy's well-being was at stake. And Christine had every resource they needed at her place. They could spread out there. And they could eat at their leisure while they worked, without interruption.

They were going to win. Brad wasn't really concerned about that. But neither was he going to go into court without every case history and statistic he could possibly have at his disposal.

With Kim Maplewood's blessing they'd moved to terminate Shawn Maplewood's parental rights. Jason didn't know. He still missed his dad. He'd be told enough to understand the decision only after the judge ruled in their favor. Just in case he didn't. It all made good, logical sense.

He and Christine had a drink over dinner and she laughed at something he said. An easy, free, appreciative laugh.

Her place, a new, five-bedroom custom house in a gated community, still managed to feel like a home. In spite of the fact that she lived there all alone.

And when his hand brushed her arm as he handed her a 2010 copy of the Rules Governing Illinois, he jerked back as though he'd been stung. Because she wasn't Jane. Which was just wrong.

Christine's questioning gaze met his. He didn't look away for a long time. Long enough to confuse him. He was a grown man alone with a woman who hadn't made any attempt to hide her desire for him. A man free to pursue his needs.

Brad dropped the textbook. Picked up his pen. Glanced down the checklist on the legal pad in front of him. Then raised his gaze to Christine.

"I can't commit to anything." The words lacked his usual finesse. "I don't want to get involved with you."

"Then there's no problem, right? If, as you say, you don't want me?"

Who'd said that? He was human. She was beautiful and she wanted him. He hadn't had sex in weeks. "I didn't say that."

The air hung with tension.

She'd been honest and up-front with him from the beginning and deserved the same in return. "I can't allow myself." Though why that was, he wasn't sure. He'd never had a problem having sex before—as long as the woman agreed that it was nothing more than a mutually satisfying interlude.

But now another woman was carrying his child.

"You do want me, then." She didn't move any closer, didn't do anything that could be construed as a come-on.

"You're an attractive woman."

"The world is filled with attractive women. Do you want them all?" She unfastened the top few buttons of her blouse.

"I enjoy the time we spend together."

"So what's the problem?"

"I don't love you."

"I know that."

"Then…"

"I'm not trying to talk you into anything. I just know that we've got the possibility of something nice going here. Nicer than I've ever known. I'd hate to pass up a great opportunity just because things aren't perfect."

"And what happens when I leave?"

"I expect we both find someone else. And, I hope, remain friends."

What irony cursed a man with a body that could feel

desire for a woman he didn't love and then suddenly rack him with guilt?

What the hell was going on?

JANE WAS STILL sitting in a state of suspended belief with ice on her chin when she heard another knock on her door.

"No," she said quietly. And then again louder. She didn't rise. Didn't even take the ice from her chin. Until the knock sounded a second time and she heard, "Ms. Hamilton? This is the police. Are you in there?"

The police? Who'd called them? Had James sent them?

Was he that sure that she'd "do the right thing"?

At the third knock, she opened the door.

A young man, probably no more than twenty-three or -four, stood on the threshold, an older equally uniformed officer slightly behind him. "Ms. Hamilton?"

"Yes."

"Are you okay?"

"Of course. Why?"

"Are you alone?"

"Yes."

"If you don't mind, we need to come in, ma'am, to verify that."

"Of course," Jane repeated, stepping back.

The young man moved past them and farther into the room, checking under the beds, in the closet and in the adjoining bathroom.

Which reminded her—she hadn't emptied the tub yet.

"What happened to your chin?" the older officer asked, his eyes narrowing. His paunch made him only slightly less intimidating.

"I tripped earlier," she said shakily, nodding toward the entrance. "Knocked it against the door."

"You're sure about that."

"Yes. I hit my chin on the door." It was the truth. And even if James had pushed the door as hard as she'd thought, there was no way to prove that. No way to measure the push of a door after the fact. No grounds for her to file a complaint. She'd opened the door in the first place. He'd never raised a hand to her. And he had asked her to step back.

"All clear." The young man returned to his partner. "You sure you're okay?" he asked, eyeing Jane.

"I'm fine. What's this all about? Who called you?"

"We just had a report that you might be in trouble," the young officer said while the older gentleman continued to watch her.

So James *had* called them? Even in spite of the trouble it could have caused him, she wasn't all that surprised. The man was a absolute master of manipulation. She saw that now. He'd make certain that she felt cared for. It was the only way he could count on her cooperation.

And he'd be his usual charming, convincing, good ol' boys' club self with the police, too. If he came face-to-face with them.

"What did I do, Officers? I know I shouldn't have been here, but I care about her. Had to make sure she was all right after getting so sick this morning. She opened the door. I didn't have a key. I didn't turn the knob. She was closer than I knew. It was an accident. She tripped...."

With a last glance around, the officers apologized for bothering her and left.

Jane very carefully closed and locked the door.

CHAPTER EIGHTEEN

7:20 p.m. May 12, 2010
Chandler, Ohio

I WAS BEING STUPID, I knew. But I didn't really care much. Sometimes, it turned out that stupid was the best way to be.

After the police had reported back that Jane Hamilton was fine, I'd asked Sheila for Ms. Hamilton's cell number. She'd given it to me, along with her room number out at the highway motel. I could have called.

But if I'd called, Ms. Hamilton would've told me she was fine—if she'd answered at all. She probably would've told me not to come. Something told me not to give her that chance.

I had to knock three times before she came to the door. "Who is it?" she called. And I noticed that someone had stuck a wad of gum over the peephole. Recently, I guessed, by the look of it. I'm a woman who lives alone. I tend to notice these things. I also saw that the curtains were drawn.

"Kelly Chapman." I raised my voice enough to be heard.

I half expected her to call out that she was busy. Or ready for bed. Anything to get rid of me.

Imagine my shock when, instead, she opened the door. Shock that only increased as I faced the visibly shaken version of the most self-possessed woman I'd ever met.

Like I'd said, sometimes stupid was the best way to be.

"Come, sit down," I said, entering the room and locking the door behind me while maintaining eye contact with Jane's lost gaze. All I could see were those eyes, seeking...I wasn't sure what yet. Seeking me, somehow.

Blindly, I reached for her hand and knew we were in trouble when she let me lead her to one of the two chairs beside a round table in front of the window.

"James was here," I said, continuing to let my instincts guide me—hoping I wasn't making a mistake.

Jane's expression was one of anguish, more than fear. And when I saw her in full light, I stared at the slightly swollen red mark on her chin and my stomach sank.

But I wasn't surprised.

BRAD DIDN'T GET Jane's message until hours after she'd called. By then she'd left a second one, telling him she was going to bed.

Listening to her voice again via his Bluetooth as he drove from home to his office just after dawn, Brad couldn't shake the unease that had plagued him all night long. There'd been something different about her voice.

It was the tone, not her words, that had him dialing her cell phone this early in the morning.

If she had to be in court this morning, she'd be up by now.

He'd spoken with her less than twelve hours ago and she'd been fine. Tired, but fine. Had something happened with the baby? But she'd have said so. Not just told him she was going to bed.

Something was wrong with him. Seriously wrong. Ever since Jane had told him she was pregnant.

No…before that. Since he'd had sex with her. He wasn't thinking clearly where she was concerned. Had turned into a worrywart.

Brad pushed speed dial for Jane four times on the short drive to work and a fifth time when he got there. And again just before going into court, leaving messages.

She was supposed to have been in her room until she went to court this morning. She could be in the shower, he guessed. Or someone might have come to take her to breakfast and she couldn't hear her cell in her purse. But if he hadn't heard from her by the time he got out of court, he was going to call the Chandler police.

JANE NODDED at Charlene, the receptionist, as she entered the offices of Brad's law firm the next morning. She'd managed to cover the bruise on her chin with makeup, but it would be harder to camouflage the wince a smile would cause.

"Is he in yet?" she asked.

"He's in court. Should be back soon. You can go in and wait if you'd like."

If the receptionist thought it odd that Jane was there on a workday morning in jeans and a cotton blouse, she gave no indication. Like Brad, and normally Jane, too, she was the consummate professional. Thanking her, Jane made her way down the hall. She saw herself safely ensconced on the dark leather couch in Brad's office with the door closed before she let her guard fall. Her left wrist, which was fine as long as she didn't use it, lay on the pillow on her lap.

She wasn't thinking much, just sitting there, waiting. She couldn't think much. She had to talk to Brad.

Where he'd been the night before didn't matter. Even if he'd been with Christine when Jane had called, needing him so badly...

"Jane?" He burst into the office, her name on his lips even before the door was fully open. "Charlene said you were here. Honey, what's going on? Where have you been? I've been..."

He'd reached the couch by then and was staring at her.

"What happened?" It was the softness of his voice that did her in. The kindness. Were all men kind when they were hurting you?

No. Wait. That was one of those random thoughts Kelly Chapman had warned her about. The insidiousness of them made them dangerous and Jane needed to dismiss them.

When she had herself under control and as ready as she was going to be, Jane looked up again, meeting Brad's concerned stare.

He wasn't James. The thought was more an acknowledgment of a well-known truth than a realization.

He wasn't James.

He was her Brad.

Jane's eyes flooded with tears, but she knew what she had to do. Looking him straight in the eye, she said aloud something she'd just admitted to herself the night before. "I'm a victim of spousal abuse."

SINKING ONTO THE COUCH beside Jane, Brad heard her words reverberate around the office as though on loudspeaker repeat. *I'm a victim of spousal abuse.*

He experienced a rage he'd never encountered within

himself, never even known it was possible to feel. He'd kill the bastard. He'd hunt him down and kill him with his bare hands.

"What happened?" he asked again when he could trust himself to speak softly. He couldn't see any bruising on her chin, but it was swollen. The cleft he knew so well was nonexistent. She had to hurt like hell.

He wanted to hold her. And she felt like a stranger.

"You mean my chin?" she asked, almost as though she'd forgotten about the injury.

"Yeah." And any other injuries he had yet to find out about. Like…God, no…had James raped her?

It took every ounce of self-control Brad had to stay in his seat at that thought. Only the need he was reading in her eyes kept him in place.

She'd been assaulted. She needed nurturing and reassurance. Security. And she'd come to him.

He could deal with his own rage after he knew she was okay.

Jane was still looking at him, but had not yet spoken. She just sat there with that pillow perched oddly on her lap.…

"Jane?"

"I…tripped and hit my chin on the door," she said, sounding more like her old self. Then she shook her head. "No," she said, still shaking slowly, and Brad got just plain scared. "No, well, that's kind of what happened, but…"

"Did someone hit you?" he asked, calling on his lawyer persona to get him through. Think, man. Don't feel.

"No," she said, her gaze clearing. "No, I hit it on the door, but not because I tripped." Her gaze dropped. Her shoulders dropped. And then, as though she was consciously gearing herself, she took a breath that seemed to inflate her again.

"I tripped, but after the door hit me. After James shoved the door into me."

"Where was this? Why was James anywhere near you?"

"My motel room. He came to my motel room last night."

With slow, halting statements, almost as though she had to consciously form each word one after the other, Jane told him about her ex-husband's visit.

"He was manipulating me, Brad. All those years... He says he just happened to see Sheila drop me off, but I don't believe that anymore."

Dark eyes wide, and with her hair in a simple ponytail, Jane looked more like a lost child than a successful woman of thirty-two.

"James knew the power he had over me and he used it. Just like always. He's a smart man. A dangerously smart man. He was my teacher. My mentor. My example and my support."

She wasn't talking about her current injuries. Jane had been an abused wife during her marriage.

Just as he'd feared.

Jane volunteered at the shelter, she wrote articles and helped other women, all to hide her own trauma. Brad didn't know whether to rejoice in Jane's newfound freedom or to cry.

A tear fell onto the pillow on her lap.

"I'm a fraud."

Of course she wasn't.

"I... It's like I don't even know myself," she continued. "How could I have been so brainwashed? How could I not have seen? How could I let myself down this way?"

The pain on her face when she raised her head slashed through him—and through every rational thought he'd been trying to have when he so desperately needed to take her away and hold her close to him for the rest of their lives.

"I knew better," she said. "I'm the strong one, the one who helps them all."

"That's still true."

"No, it's not. I'm weak, Brad. The worst kind of coward. I've been hiding from myself. What kind of example am I? Except as one of hopelessness and failure. A person who couldn't get away even after I was free," she said. And then, with a sniffle and a ragged sigh, she continued. "Last night Kelly Chapman tried to convince me that it wasn't my fault—that the mind has coping mechanisms and that I'm to be commended for mine. But the cold truth is that I was hiding."

Starting to feel sick, Brad reached for Jane's hand.

"Ouch!" she cried, pulling her arm more closely into her body.

And he caught a glimpse of the wrist her sleeve had been covering. With a raised brow he looked at it, then her.

"I caught myself with my wrist when I fell."

"Have you seen a doctor?"

"No. It's okay."

"It's pretty swollen."

"I know, but it's not broken. I can move it. Besides…"

"Besides…what?"

"I know what broken bones feel like."

"The bastard!"

"Yeah." With a fresh spate of tears she nodded again. "He had me convinced, when he dropped the weight on my foot, that it was my fault because he'd told me to move. We'd been cleaning out the closet in the spare room when it happened. I'd been insisting on keeping an appointment in New York the next morning, but he wanted me home. The next thing I knew I was writhing in pain and he was on his knees at my feet. He kept saying he told me to move, kept asking why I hadn't. He was compassionate and contrite, tending to me so gently that I wasn't sure what had happened. I promised I was only bruised, pretended, even to myself, that although the injury was painful, it wasn't serious. I spared him the guilt of having hurt me. He was so kind as he swore that if I'd only moved, I'd have been fine. He hated to see me hurt. He was so certain that his recollection of the timing was correct and I was in shock from the pain.

"He was incredibly attentive for the next couple of weeks, spoiling me rotten. And I missed my appointment in New York, just like he wanted."

Brad held back as much emotion as was humanly possible. It took every bit of strength he had. He couldn't bear to hear any more, and yet he had to know. Had to be her support.

"Was that the only time he hurt you other than the tennis court and the stairs? I'm assuming those police reports were closed with suspicion for a reason."

"Yes, I guess they were. And no, those weren't the only times."

She told him about an incident on a set of stairs at the university. And another time, when her hand had been shut in a car door he'd opened for her. "Were you planning a trip to New York, then, too?"

"No. But I'd asked him a question about Lee Anne. At

that point, I thought she was just a student who'd gone on one of his New England tours. But I was pretty sure I'd seen her drive by the house and that he'd waved to her. Anyway, my hand didn't need medical attention and he was so sympathetic and sweet, insisting on doing everything for me, that the whole issue went away. I'd forgotten all about it until last night."

"Which was exactly what he wanted."

"Yeah. And the way Kelly Chapman explained it, his behavior was also a matter of control. He had to make certain that I was still able to be manipulated. His ability to get me to believe him gave him power and a sense of security."

"Things everyone needs."

"Right. But James gets them in an unhealthy way."

There were a couple of other incidents, as well. And each one depended on timing. The fall that had been reported to the police had happened as she and James were walking downstairs together. She'd sped up and stepped on his foot, which had unbalanced her. In retrospect, she was fairly certain he'd slowed down. She'd just been telling him she'd won an award at the magazine.

"So what changed your perspective? Did you call Dr. Chapman? Was she able to help you see what James had been doing?"

"She put it all together for me, but I was already starting to get it. He'd said something about Lee Anne slipping in the tub. Having two accident-prone wives seemed too coincidental. And then I remembered the time on the stairs in the university. I knew something was drastically wrong, so I pretended to agree with him so he'd leave. Funny, it was the baby that opened my eyes."

"The baby?"

"Before, I was the only one affected, and since James never hit me, never did anything overt enough for me to press charges, I fell right into his trap—an unknowing victim to the manipulation. Especially after I went to Victim Witness and they told me that the stories I recounted to them did not suggest abuse.

"But last night, when James knocked me down, when I considered what could have happened to our baby if I hadn't caught my fall..."

She swallowed, then continued, "I just saw things differently. It wasn't about James anymore, or about keeping peace. I didn't even care if he was right. All I knew was that I had to protect the baby—and that there was something that I needed to protect the baby against."

"You'd never thought you were worth protecting when it was just you?"

"I guess not. Kelly pointed that out last night. That, plus the fact that I no longer cared who was right or what the truth really was. In other words, because the only thing that mattered to me was the safety of the baby, I was outside James's control. No longer vulnerable to his manipulation."

"He no longer had a hold over you."

"That's right."

"Will you see Dr. Chapman again?"

"Maybe. Probably. She gave me her number so I can call if I get into a rough spot.

"There's something else, Brad. James wrote those notes. We'll probably never be able to prove it. He's so good at covering his deeds, but I know he wrote them."

"He told you?"

"Yes, not that he'll ever admit that. But I knew,

anyway. He told me he knew I'd do the right thing. That was what he'd always told me. It became our moniker, something I now see that he used to control me. To manipulate me like I was some kind of Pavlovian dog. If James told me to do the right thing, I'd do what he wanted. Because, of course, what he wanted was always the right thing. And said he knew I'd get the message. That I always did."

Do the right thing. The exact words in the anonymous messages...

If James had admitted to threatening Jane, and if James was back in custody, then that was one less worry.... "But they started before you were even involved with the case," Brad reminded both of them.

"Yes, but not before James knew that he was in trouble and that they were going to call me. He was first arrested a couple of weeks before I heard from Sheila."

"He was so certain you'd get his message."

"Right."

"But you didn't."

Jane didn't say anything, her gaze thoughtful. "Which means that you had already escaped the hold he had over you, sweetie. Already immune..."

"Or that I'd just buried the abuse so deeply, I couldn't see it."

"Have you called Detective Thomas?" Jane was out of danger. What a relief.

Jane paused, and Brad's tension returned.

"No."

CHAPTER NINETEEN

"AT THIS POINT, only you and Kelly Chapman know anything about this. My conversation with Kelly was confidential." Jane expected Brad to react as Kelly Chapman initially had to this part. The therapist had looked at her with compassion and pity. As though Jane wasn't healed yet, but she'd get there.

But there was more to it than that. "I wouldn't let her tell anyone what I told her. I'm not pressing charges."

"You didn't even expose the bastard?"

"No."

"You have to, Jane. You know that." His frustration was evident. But then he was a lawyer. He'd spent all of his adult life believing in the judicial process.

"I do know, but will you listen to me please?" She lifted her arms to punctuate her request and cursed as she immediately dropped her left arm back down to the pillow.

Without a word Brad rose, walked over to a cupboard outside his private bath. Still saying nothing, he returned with a stretch bandage and tenderly wrapped her wrist.

It was a testament to the needy fool she'd become that the touch of Brad's fingers made her want to curl up in his lap, safe and sound forever.

"We need to have that looked at when we're done

here," he said, setting her wrist back on the pillow. Jane let the statement stand.

"You asked me to listen," he said, reclaiming his seat beside her. The action may have been small, but it said a lot to her.

"First," she started, "the judge declared a mistrial." After explaining what details she'd been given the night before, from Kelly first and then Sheila, Jane continued. "That gives me some time."

"Time for him to come after you?"

"He's not going to do that, Brad. Think about it. For now, James believes I'm still under his control. Or I would have pressed charges. Don't you see? And if I had, with his rich wife, he likely would've posted bail again. My injuries are minor and it would be my word against his. Even the letters probably wouldn't be enough to hold him, since no one else heard him confess. If I pressed charges he'd know he didn't have me and then he'd be desperate to get me back under his control. Just look at what happened to Lee Anne. As long as James feels like he's in charge, I'm safe.

"Besides, I still have my posse watching over me here."

When Jane had presented her theory to Kelly Chapman late the night before, the psychologist had agreed that it made sense.

"I hate to admit it, but you're probably right. For now, you'll be safer this way." Brad responded almost identically to the doctor.

Thank God she hadn't completely lost her ability to reason. She hadn't been unconsciously finding a way to justify letting James off the hook again.

"I need the time for another reason," she told Brad.

"And I need to be certain that nothing we've talked about today will leave this room."

As soon as she heard the words, fear ripped through Jane.

"You're asking if you can trust me?"

Crazy, wasn't it? "I guess I am."

Brad sat back, and then his expression eased. "How could you not have doubts at this point? About everyone?" he mused. "After all you've been through, all you've been forced to acknowledge in the past twenty-four hours."

"I don't trust my judgment," she said aloud. *You're too hard on yourself. You don't love yourself enough.* Dr. Chapman's words repeated in her mind.

She still hadn't digested that one. She had quite a good opinion of herself. Or so she'd thought, at least in some contexts. And that was a key point. When it came to work, to skill, to writing ability—she was confident. But when it came to relationships, to love—she didn't know who she was.

"I need your advice," she said now, wishing that they could go back a couple of months and be best friends again. Wishing that they didn't have to deal with the awkwardness of having a baby together.

And yet...

She couldn't think of anyone else she'd ever want to be the father of her child.

"You know I'll help in any way I can," he said, looking quite professional all of a sudden in his gray slacks and jacket and sedately striped tie. The clothes hadn't changed. Had he? Or was she the only who felt so different?

"I...I'm just not sure how to handle all of this in terms of my career." She had no idea how she was going to handle it personally, either, but there was time for that. "I've made a career out of supporting other women. All of the promotion we've done since the launch of *Twenty-Something* has been centered around having a strong woman at the helm—me. We used me as a brand, to make the readers' attachment to the magazine more personal. I'm the example of what all women can be. I'm the quintessential strong woman. The one who is fully aware, who has the strength to face life head-on. I'm the woman who has her eyes wide open and my success is the prize every woman can aspire to—and reach. If it gets out that I was a victim who didn't help herself, I could lose all credibility."

"Maybe with some." She'd known Brad would be honest with her.

"Our readers relate me to the magazine, Brad. You know that. You've read the letters I get. And then there's Kim and all the other women I've known at the shelter over the years."

Because work was something she could think about, she was thinking about it a lot. But then, she'd always thought of it a lot. She'd always put work first. At least she had since James. He'd claimed she had when she'd been married to him.

"Not only could it ruin my career, but what about all of the women out there that I've helped, and could continue to help? They look up to me, believe me when I tell them that they don't have to be victims. If even one of them gave up, I'd never be able to forgive myself. Hasn't James already done enough damage?"

"I don't…"

"I saw the look on your face when I first told you. You felt sick, didn't you? Like I was different, somehow."

"Okay, yes, but only for a moment. And not in the way you think."

"Because you know the real me. Most people don't. How could they? I've been hiding away. Even from myself.

"And on top of that, I'm pregnant," she exclaimed as the weight came hurtling down on her again. Not that the pregnancy had any bearing on her credibility. Maybe on her intelligence for having unprotected sex, but...

"I don't think—"

"I feel like such a fraud." She didn't know herself. And worse. "I'm not sure I like myself anymore," she said slowly, watching Brad as though somewhere in his expression was the key. To what she didn't know.

"Why?" he asked, his whole countenance bland. "Because you've just discovered that you're human like the rest of us?"

How such soft words could have such impact Jane didn't know. Neither could she get enough breath to respond.

"You hold yourself to impossibly high standards. You know that, right?"

"And I live up to them."

"Do you?"

Most of the time she did. That was who she was. She promised and then delivered. She did what she said she was going to do and she always gave her best.

"I can't deal with this right now."

"I thought you said you wanted my advice."

"Not about this." She couldn't take criticism. Not now and especially not from him.

"Then what?"

I don't know. I can't explain my feelings. I just needed you. And here I am.

"I need to know what to say in court. How do I handle this in such a way that James gets what he deserves, without anyone else getting hurt?"

Brad's eyes narrowed. "Let me ask you this. What do you think James Todd deserves?"

"I don't know."

"Do you think, after all you've discovered, that he could've killed Lee Anne?"

She hadn't been married to a murderer.

Before the thought had even fully surfaced, Jane froze. This wasn't about James at all. Her belief in who he was, her assurance in her deposition that James wasn't capable of killing—it had never been about James. It was about her. About facing the fact that she might have been married to a murderer. She might have made a choice that was that horribly wrong.

"I don't know if he killed her," she finally said. "But I think he could've done so. The facts fit. He was angry, and an accident happened..."

James's method of operation—make it look like an accident. Convince everyone that it was an accident. Especially the victim.

"You already know what I'm going to tell you."

Of course she did, which was probably why she'd come to him. At least in part. "To tell the truth."

"And when they ask if he ever deliberately hurt you?"

Years of conditioning didn't leave in a day. Jane had to think, really think, to know what to say. She instinctively wanted to deny it, but she knew differently. She knew what he'd done.

"Yes," she heard herself say. And resisted the urge to duck while she held back tears. She felt like a bad girl. A bad woman. But her mind told her otherwise now.

Brad's nod was confirmation.

Her own feelings, a flood of unrecognizable emotion, swamped her when she looked him straight in the eye and she couldn't handle it.

She was in crisis and she'd come to Brad.

She was looking for herself, for her foundation, and she'd come to Brad. Because he was more to her than just an ex-best friend. He was more to her than the father of her unborn child. And she had no idea what to do with that knowledge.

BRAD COULDN'T GET Jane to go to the emergency room. But he didn't really press her very hard. Like her, he was fairly certain that her wrist wasn't broken, and she clearly wasn't ready to answer the questions that the doctors would ask. Or to face the reporting they were required to do.

But he did insist that she contact Detective Thomas, who, within an hour, had spoken with Sheila Grant, who'd requested the threatening letters to use as evidence against James Todd. For now, until the new trial date was set and upon them, they agreed with Jane. For her safety, James wasn't to know she'd turned him in.

Brad insisted on one other thing, as well—that Jane allow him to help her do the things she couldn't do easily with a hurt wrist. It was a testament to how badly Jane's world was off-kilter that, without even a hint of demurring, she agreed to his nearly constant presence.

Until Christine called. He'd completely forgotten the other woman. Forgotten that she'd told him she'd call as soon as she had their court time for the morning.

He'd taken his phone off his belt when he'd been cleaning Pet's cage after bringing Jane back home, her driver right behind them, and had forgotten to put it back on. He was standing at the stove when it rang. Jane was closest to the counter where the phone lay, his screen—and caller ID—in plain sight.

"It's okay," Jane said, grabbing the spoon he was using to stir the homemade spaghetti sauce. "Talk to her. I can do this."

She'd behaved perfectly naturally, as nonchalant as always. So why did he feel as though a curtain had come down between them? One that he didn't want there.

And why did he resent Christine's interruption? His women had never affected him and Jane. There was no logical reason that they would—baby or no. He and Jane had only ever been just friends. That was all they'd ever be.

She turned and the expression on her face was neutral. Bordering on fake.

And Brad silently cursed Christine for calling.

What in the hell was going on?

The call was short. *How are you? The work's delivered. Goodbye.* Christine's feelings would be hurt. He knew he'd been rude.

And Jane thought *she* was a fraud.

"IF THERE'S NO OTHER EVIDENCE that James is abusive—and Lee Anne's autopsy didn't show any evidence of bruising or contusions, by the way—then my testimony alone wouldn't be enough to convict him, right?" Jane was chattering through dinner, pretending his phone had never rung. Pretending that she wasn't jealous of Christine Ryan.

"As a character witness, you'd be showing the jury a history of manipulative abuse by the way of supposed accidents. You'd be showing them a husband capable of harming his wife."

She had no right to be jealous. No ties to Brad—other than the fact that she was having his baby.

"But what if it was just me? I wasn't good for him. I was too strong, too independent. I challenged him constantly. What he did to me wasn't right, I get that, but does it make him capable of killing someone else?" She had to be able to live with herself.

"You see what you're doing, don't you?"

She wanted to think strategy. Deal with the physical pain rather than the emotional intricacies. Her wrist, lying wrapped in her lap, hardly hurt at all. Her chin, on the other hand, hurt every time she opened her mouth.

James left reminders.

The look in Brad's eye wouldn't let her run.

"I'm backtracking," she said, appetite gone. "Thinking of James. Protecting him. Still being a victim."

Brad nodded.

FOR A MAN WHO ALWAYS HAD a plan, Brad was acting highly out of character, just hanging around. He'd done the dishes since Jane could hardly do them with one hand. And he'd put Pet's blanket over her cage for the night, in case Jane was able to sleep in in the morning. She wasn't due to the office until noon.

"It's nine o'clock. I should go," he said. He'd checked the trash. It was only half-full, but he'd emptied it anyway.

Jane was leaning against the kitchen counter, her arms folded across her chest, with her left wrist resting on top.

"Why don't you go have your shower and then I'll rewrap that."

"Okay. Thanks." She was gone without argument.

And Brad spent the next fifteen minutes trying not

to imagine her naked. Trying not to remember every detail of those legs spread open before him. Trying not to think about the fact that Christine had called and he'd wanted to tell her she had no right invading the space he shared with Jane. Which made no sense at all.

Two months ago he'd been basically carefree, with a date and a lover when he wanted one, a friend who was around when they had time for each other.

And now...

He was a man spending far too much time thinking about his friend, not enough time thinking about dates, and he was going to be a father. Committed to another human being for the rest of his life. How had his life become so confusing? More important, what in the hell was he going to do about it?

"I was thinking about names for the baby." Jane's voice accompanied her arrival down the hall from her bedroom. She was out of the shower and he'd managed to stay in the living room.

Names for the baby. What about a name for the mess they'd created? They were going to have to figure out what they were going to do with each other. About each other.

They weren't really friends anymore. Things were too awkward between them. Even though they'd created a child, they'd never been lovers. And she was pretty much all he thought about.

"Rachel if it's a girl. Rachel Marie. And Timothy Robert if it's a boy," Jane continued, rambling on about something so far removed from them, in that moment, that he barely heard her.

He was beginning to realize that avoidance wasn't an answer to life's problems. But he'd be damned if he knew what was.

"What do you think?" Jane, dressed in blue fleece lounging pajamas, had stopped about three feet short of where he stood by the fireplace mantel, looking at the miniature jeweled globe he'd bought her for Christmas. The elastic bandage hung from her good hand.

Shoving his own hands in his pockets, he turned to her. "What about a last name?" he asked, though names were the last thing on his mind. "Whose name will the baby have?"

"Mine. The mother's name goes on the birth certificate."

"It's perfectly legal for the child to have my last name even if we're not married."

He wasn't sure why he was pushing this. Until this moment he hadn't thought about names of any description. He'd considered medical tests, finances and the lifetime obligation. But not this.

She held the bandage out to him.

"How about a compromise? If we have a girl, she'll have my last name. If we have a boy, he'll have yours."

After a second, he took the bandage. Tried not to touch her skin as he began, methodically, to wrap while his mind ran wild.

Heart pounding, Brad hooked the last metal piece. "We could make it so that we both have the same last name."

"A legal name change?"

Brad peered down into dark eyes that engulfed him. She didn't look away. "We could get married."

CHAPTER TWENTY

JANE BACKED UP into an armchair and sat down. "I can't marry you, Brad. You know that."

Especially not now. Not when her heart was laying claim to a man who'd shown no sign of wanting hers.

"Look at me," she continued. "I've just realized that the man I was married to was abusing me and making me believe he wasn't. I thought I was thinking my own thoughts, but I was thinking his, even though I'm a capable, intelligent woman. Right now I don't trust my own mind enough to testify in court, let alone get married."

"You were the perfect victim for someone in a position of authority but secretly suffering from low self-esteem, someone who needs to be constantly adored and yet never trusts that he *is* adored."

Jane hadn't thought of it that way—but Brad's description of James was pretty accurate.

"In the first place," he continued, still standing, with his hands back in his pockets. "You were his student, and he was a professor in your major subject, making you even more likely to let him shape your mind."

Yes.

"And with your stepbrother states away and your mother out on a boat for most of the year, you had no family around to watch your back. Or to notice if anything was amiss."

"And our friends were all James's friends," she added. "People who were older than me and saw me more as one of his students than his wife."

"And your work life was in another state from your home life," Brad added. "A separate community where I'm suspecting you were a completely different person."

"Which was why my career was so threatening to him. And why I was able to succeed at my career, because he wasn't there pulling me down."

Realizations had been crashing down on her for twenty-four hours now. Helped greatly by Kelly Chapman's gentle guidance. And probably by the fact that Jane desperately wanted to see the truth.

"All of this still leaves me a load of emotional baggage to sort through."

"Where does us getting married play into that?"

There were tears in her eyes as she looked up at him. "We aren't in love."

At least one of them wasn't. And she hoped to God neither of them were, hoped that her sudden attraction to Brad Manchester was just her mind playing tricks on her again.

But she'd let him touch her. She'd let him enter her. For two years she'd spent all of her free time with him—confided in him. And when her world collapsed, he was the one she'd needed.

"Maybe that's the answer," he said. "Look at all of the love matches that end up in divorce. I see it every single day. Divorce statistics in this country are off the scale. Fifty percent of first marriages fail."

"So why get married?"

"A marriage of convenience could work. It might

even have a better chance at working because there aren't false expectations to live up to. To let down."

He didn't love her enough—not the once-in-a-lifetime kind of love he'd spoken of. She'd known that.

Swallowing, Jane put on her work face. Hid behind the walls she'd built during her marriage. "Is that honestly what you want? Or are you just grappling here because we don't know what to do?"

Was she willing to settle? To become his next Emily? No, she wasn't. Jane didn't need to be married. Especially not to a man who could never love her.

"Right now, I don't honestly know," Brad said, sounding as weary as he suddenly looked, standing there. Had those lines around his eyes appeared in the past weeks? "I'm still trying to adjust to the fact that I'm going to be a dad."

"What about Christine?" And any future Christines?

Her baby was going to have other women in and out of his life—mothering him. It felt horrible. But, as Brad said, statistically, split families weren't out of the ordinary. Kids having two homes, two sets of parents.

"I can't seem to generate enough interest," Brad said, his expression pinched.

"Maybe you aren't trying hard enough."

If she couldn't have him, she had to send him away, before she did something stupid like ask him to stay. To hold her. Lie with her in her bed and run those magical hands all over her body. Try to love her.

BRAD HIKED ALONE on Saturday on a trail he'd never taken before. A deserted, barren path that asked only that he sweat and work his muscles to the point of soreness. He complied. If there were trees, he didn't see them. If the sun danced with plants and together cast shadow figures, he didn't notice.

Turning his attention inward, Brad felt the pain of the exercise and found the determination to make it to the top of the trail. And then to make it back down again.

He had a date with Christine that evening. They'd talked both Thursday and Friday nights, but he hadn't seen her.

Dressed in fresh jeans and a button-down oxford, he showed up at her door five minutes late.

They were renting a bicycle built for two for an hour's ride along Lake Michigan and then having dinner someplace that struck their fancy.

Plans for a perfect evening.

"You look fantastic," he said, viewing her long legs in fashionably tight denim, the white blouse with tails hanging out below a black vest. Her hair, usually curled around her shoulders, was up in a clip.

"Thank you, sir. So do you." She reached up for a kiss. A quick touch. And then it was done.

He drove to the bike shop and paid for the bike. They picked their trail, chatting the entire time—about many things. The breeze off the lake was kind, for once, with enough of a hint of warmth left from the day's sunshine to keep them comfortable.

Dinner was equally nice. Great food. Great company.

It was no surprise when they ended up back at her place. Or that she poured glasses of wine and headed straight to the master suite.

She handed him a glass. "To us," she said.

"To us." He clinked her glass, but didn't drink just yet.

The only time he'd been in Jane's bedroom with her, she'd been sick.

Taking off her vest, Christine unbuttoned her blouse, exposing her satin bra.

Lying on her side across the end of the bed, her head propped on one hand, her glass of wine in the other, she said, "Let's have it, cowboy."

She wasn't talking about sex.

"I...don't belong here."

"Says who?" She looked around. "Yep, this is my place. And I'm here. Wanting you here..."

Brad stood still, knowing where this was going. He could bury his fingers in her hair, lose himself in her welcoming passion, fall into an exhausted sleep. And wake up sometime in the night in the arms of a beautiful woman, instead of home alone in his cold and lonely bed.

Brad stepped back. Not much. But enough.

"My heart isn't in it," he said. If there was a way to refuse a woman kindly, he hadn't found it.

"It's okay, Brad." Her eyes were serious. "We don't need heart here. Only mutual desire."

She was reciting the rules of his own game. And they didn't set well.

She stood. Walked over to him. Reached up to kiss him.

"No." Pulling back, Brad moved to the dresser, set down his glass of wine. "You're gorgeous. And entertaining." *And if I had a working brain cell I'd be on that bed with you in an instant.*

"But I can't do this. I'm... I guess I'm not a free man."

The words were wrong. But for the first time in weeks, Brad felt completely right.

Christine sipped her wine, but didn't cover herself. "It's Jane, isn't it?"

No. Of course not. It was just the whole baby thing.

"Yes." His mouth betrayed him. "I guess it is."

"Have you slept with her yet?"

He deserved that; Jane did not.

"A decent man doesn't kiss and tell." Another line from his repertoire that he wasn't proud of.

She didn't push any further and he'd known she wouldn't. Christine didn't expect him to be here for the long haul. Maybe she didn't even want him long-term. Either way, it didn't make a difference. He knew now that he was no longer open to a quick fling any more than he was to a committed relationship.

He'd rather be alone.

And with that realization, he turned to go.

"My door is open if you change your mind," Christine said. "You're a man in a million, Brad Manchester. So much so that, for once, I was willing to settle for being second best."

"And you, Christine, are one very classy woman. Don't ever settle for being second best," Brad said as he gave her one last look and then took himself home to shower.

CHAPTER TWENTY-ONE

WHEN MAY LEFT, it took Jane's morning sickness with it. June brought heat, a too-healthy appetite and sweating. Her wrist had healed. Her chin had healed. Jane noticed every little and not-so-little change in her body. She even accepted and tended to her sudden addiction to hamburgers with extra mustard. She'd always hated mustard.

Sheila Grant and the Chandler police hadn't found any connection between the threats she'd received and James Todd, but in the weeks since he'd come to her motel room in Chandler, she hadn't received another one.

Thomas now considered the case closed. *Twenty-Something* was continuing with the extra security for at least another month.

The baby had become Jane's future. The baby and work.

Jane told her boss about the baby. Barbara already knew about the trial. Jane had offered to help find someone else for her position if Barbara felt the fallout from Jane's testimony was going to jeopardize the credibility of *Twenty-Something* in any way. A spokesperson who could appear to be a fraud wouldn't sell magazines. She told Barbara that she'd do any and all publicity required to turn over the reins to another role model, a better adjusted figure with whom readers could identify.

So many people had relied on her as they invested money and careers, lives, in the risk of starting up a new national magazine. She hadn't lived up to their expectations.

Barbara had told her to wait and see. To handle the situations as she thought best and to keep her apprised of any negative responses. They'd reassess after the third quarter to see if there were noticeable financial ramifications and go from there.

Jane had called Brad with the news. He'd been in the city and had taken her out for a hamburger, extra mustard and nothing else, to celebrate.

She saw him regularly these days. He'd appointed himself overseer of her doctor's orders. Her doctor had recommended exercise and so they developed a routine together. But he never stayed long. And never talked about his life outside of her and the baby.

She didn't ask what he was doing these days. Not knowing hurt less. Let her stay distant and keep her heart somewhat to herself. She was headed for trouble where he was concerned. She knew that, but couldn't stop herself from spending as much time with him as she could. He was the father of her unborn child.

Kim and Jason Maplewood had had their hearing. Shawn Maplewood's visiting rights had been permanently revoked. In the end, Jason had taken the news well. Kim enrolled him in a Big Brothers program and Jason loved all the attention he was getting. Shawn had relocated to another state, moving in with a woman he'd met on the Internet.

Jane had heard about it all when she'd run into Kim at Durango where Jane was still volunteering and Kim was a frequent visitor. Brad hadn't even told her they'd been to court.

She never went to his home or visited his office. But she'd told him about the meeting she'd scheduled with her senior staff that third Wednesday in June. She'd just passed the three-month mark and was beginning to lose her perfectly flat stomach.

"Thank you all for coming." Dressed in a pink linen suit, she stood at the head of the conference table.

Sam and Donna were there, because they were lead writer and photographer respectively. As were her three-member editorial staff, her production and marketing managers, the head of accounting and *Twenty-Something*'s on-staff attorney. She'd handpicked each of them for their jobs, and for their place in that day's meeting.

As she met their curious gazes, her smile faltered. *I can't do it. I just can't do it.* Her hair was down around her shoulders as was usual for work, but she'd curled it that morning. As if that made a difference.

You have nothing to be ashamed of. She remembered Kelly Chapman's words from one of their four phone sessions over the past month. *You were hurt and your mind saved you the only way it could. It got you out and on to a new life. Keep looking. It's ready to tell you all. You've always been honest with yourself. You'll see that.*

Someone cleared his throat. Someone else coughed. Sam tapped the end of his pencil against a pad of paper over and over again, creating a rhythm that boomed into the room. Donna laid a hand on top of it. He grimaced and mouthed an apology

Jane took a deep breath. "This is very difficult for me."

She could feel every single gaze in the room on her, making her sweat.

"You have no agenda this morning." She stated the obvious. They had quarterly meetings together, all of them there in that room at once and she always passed out the agenda a week ahead of time.

"And this isn't the end of a quarter."

She sounded robotic even though she'd chosen her words so carefully. She'd written them down. All she had to do was read them.

If she had a chance in hell of pulling off her plan, she was going to have to have the support of every single person in that room. It was a lot to ask. And for what? They'd have their jobs regardless of who was at the helm of *Twenty-Something*.

No. She'd been good to them. She'd given them all jobs. She was a good boss and she had a right to ask for help when she needed it. She'd repeat the words to herself for the next hundred years if that was what it took to change her thinking. Dr. Chapman didn't seem to think it would take nearly that long.

Jane didn't know what Brad thought. She was trying not to let his opinion matter so much. Trying not to need him.

"I have two orders of business. First, I'm pregnant. Second, I used to be married to an abusive man."

The room, which had been uncomfortably quiet, now became silent as a tomb. Jane's tomb.

"The baby is due in December. If he or she cooperates, I will give birth during the month of our shutdown and be here, at least part-time, for January's start-up and we can sail smoothly along."

Everyone was staring at her, a couple with their mouths open. Sam wasn't even slouching in his chair.

"We already had an issue on unplanned pregnancy on the calendar for September, when all the coeds are back

in college, many away from home for the first time...."
She was rambling. Every one present was well aware
of their calendar.

"My editorial will focus on things that I draw from
personal experience, good and bad, about being single
and expecting."

Sam wrote something and turned his pad so Donna
could see, not realizing that meant Jane could read it,
too.

Who's the father? I'll kill the son of a bitch.

"Um." Jane blinked. Her lips were trembling but she
was *not* going to cry. "Brad," she said. "You've all met
Brad Manchester." He'd been to the past two Christmas
parties with her and to the July barbecues. He'd been to
her office many times, too.

Other than Sam, no one else had moved. "Brad Manchester is the baby's father." She had control of her voice
again. "And though this was definitely unplanned and
shocked us both, we're moving forward. I want the baby
very much."

"When's the wedding?" Sam's voice seemed to crack
the air in the room.

"There isn't going to be one." Before any more mur-
ders could be planned, Jane added, "My choice, not
his.

"Now, on to the second issue," she said, wishing she'd
started this meeting sitting down, as she normally did.

"Some of you know that I was married several years
ago. I was recently called to be a witness for the prosecution in my ex-husband's murder trial." She very quickly
and as briefly as possible explained the details of the
Ohio case. "And that leads me to the difficult part. You
may have noticed that I haven't been myself lately. In
the midst of the trial, I had a bit of a...breakdown." It

wasn't pretty, but it was the truth. And they had to know the truth. All of it. So Jane told them all of it. Just like she'd told Dr. Chapman. And Brad.

And Sheila Grant and Detective Thomas, too.

To their credit, no one interrupted. Not a single question was asked. She tried not to notice as a couple of people wiped away tears.

"And that brings us to the main reason for this meeting," she said, shoulders straight. "So far, news of the trial has been kept to a minimum, but I suspect that's going to change soon. The judge has recently ruled to allow testimony from Lee Anne's sister, in spite of it being hearsay, regarding the accidents that happened to her sister during her marriage to the defendant." The defendant. A third party. Kelly Chapman had suggested that viewing the situation from some distance would allow Jane to see it realistically. "The prosecution needs my testimony. At the moment, word of my…situation… is being kept under wraps. The defense knows only that I will be testifying, the changed status of the content will not be revealed until I am on the witness stand." Sheila's answer, with Detective Thomas's input, to keeping Jane safe in the meantime. Seemed things could be a little less by the book in small-town court.

"We here at *Twenty-Something* have to expect the story to hit national news. The public might be a bit desensitized to spousal murder, but add in the bigamy element and I can see the whole thing being sensationalized. Assuming no one famous dies or has an affair in the meantime."

Nods came from all around the table.

"That being said, we have to face the fact that the reputation we've built for me as a strong, successful, in-control role model to women everywhere could soon come under attack."

A strong word. Maybe too strong. But maybe not.

"Barbara Manley is fully apprised of the situation. We acknowledge that I stand to look like a fraud...."

No one moved or spoke as Jane's voice faltered.

"So," she said too loudly, trying to project an optimism she didn't feel. "Ms. Manley has determined that I am to remain in my position here at *Twenty-Something* as long as our financials aren't affected."

At work the bottom line was clear.

"Our goal is to find a way to deal with this situation, with the fact that I've built my career, and the reputation of this magazine, on being an example of a strong woman in the know. Had I started out acknowledging the abuse, and shown how I overcame it, that would be one thing. But I didn't. If our readership was only abused women, we'd have nothing to worry about—but it's not. All these years that I've been teaching women to stand up for themselves, encouraging them to get healthy, promising them that they could succeed, I've been a victim myself. I was...a victim of abuse...as recently as a month ago."

A victim. God, she hated those two words. Detested them. Hated what they made her. Hated that she was as vulnerable as everyone else? As fallible?

"That's our challenge, folks. Any suggestions?"

The room had been paralyzed, but now stirred, several voices speaking at once, throwing out ideas. Some were heard, some fell into the cacophony. One or two were picked up on, discussed by a few while others continued to brainstorm.

Where she usually was in the middle of the fray, Jane sank into her seat and waited. It took half an hour.

"It'll work," Sam said, tapping his pencil against his pad.

"Do you think this Dr. Chapman will agree to do a story?" Marge Davenport asked. It was the first direct question Jane had faced since she'd turned over the floor.

"I think so," Jane said. "Would you like me to ask?"

"If you don't mind, I can call her."

"Fine."

And just like that, Jane went from an isolated, self-reliant woman to a more fully functioning member of society.

And *Twenty-Something* would also do a special issue on the real-life story—including the trial.

JANE'S ROOM at the Chandler bed-and-breakfast was nice, a suite really, with a double bed, nightstands and a chest of drawers in one area, and through an archway, a daybed that had served as both couch and Brad's impromptu sleeping place, and a table that held the remains of their breakfast. The bathroom, shared by other guests, was down the hall.

Brad was there at his suggestion, not Jane's. Maybe she'd have asked him to accompany her but he hadn't waited to find out. Nor had he given her a chance to turn him down. He'd driven her to the airport and seen her safely off. Then been on the very next flight. As it turned out, she'd been happy to have him there.

He was guarding her room from the inside as a team of local officers took turns from the outside, while Jane tried to pretend that she was perfectly fine. They'd flown in the night before, she'd be testifying this morning, and their flight back to Chicago left at three that afternoon.

Her staff, many of whom Brad had come to know much better over the past month of interviews, would stay for the remainder of the trial.

"How do I look?" Jane came out of the room where she'd slept in the big bed alone, wearing a black skirt and gold jacket with black braided trim that he'd never seen before.

She'd mentioned not wanting to swelter under a suit in the mid-July heat.

"Great," he said, his body confirming the truth of his words. He was getting used to the phenomenon now—to a body that responded only to her. Getting used to ignoring it, that was.

"Should I wear my hair up or down?" She raised the curls off her neck, holding them at the back of her head.

Brad saw the breasts she'd just lifted. And he saw the vulnerable, struggling woman who needed a friend.

"Leave it down," he said. He figured that was what she really wanted since she'd taken the trouble to curl it. "It looks great against that jacket."

How she wore her hair didn't matter in the slightest. He knew for a fact that Jane Hamilton was gorgeous even with her hair sopping wet and straggly—the way he'd seen her at the *Twenty-Something* barbecue last summer when she'd stepped backward and fallen, fully dressed, into the pool. "You're going to do fine."

The doubt in her dark eyes clutched at him as she said, "Oh, Brad, I sure hope so. I just want this done."

"Come here."

She walked toward him, her gaze never leaving his.

"This is a new suit." He'd meant to offer deep and meaningful words of inspiration, but every time he looked at her, he got lost. He wasn't her friend anymore. He was just the father of her child. A man who...loved her.

He loved her.

"It's my first maternity outfit." She lifted the jacket enough to show him the elasticized panel in her skirt—allowing room for the slight protrusion that was his baby growing inside her. He wanted to touch her belly, but couldn't.

He loved her.

"I wonder how long it will be before I start to feel her." Her smile didn't quite reach her eyes, but it was a good effort. It took him a second to realize that she had no idea what was happening to him. Within him.

"According to the books, it'll be another month or so."

The doctor had told them the same thing the week before when they'd gone for the sixteen-week visit.

Brad searched for something—anything—to say.

He loved her.

There was a knock on the door. It was time to go.

And Brad had yet to come up with the words to see her through.

"Okay, little one, come with Mama and we'll get through this." Jane's voice was steadier than he'd heard it all morning.

And Brad knew that Jane didn't need any inspiration from him. She was the strongest, most together woman he'd ever known.

CHAPTER TWENTY-TWO

Thursday, July 15, 2010
Chandler, Ohio

I WAS SITTING with Donna Jordon, photographer with *Twenty-Something*. A woman who, like Sheila, didn't pull any punches, Donna was obviously devoted to her boss. I'd noticed that the first time I'd met her, and liked her straight off.

I'd met Marge Davenport, *Twenty-Something*'s senior editor, as well. And spent a good bit of time with Sam, who was doing most of the writing for the special August issue of *Twenty-Something*. I enjoyed my interviews with Sam. He was different. Smart and interesting. And so well adjusted, emotionally speaking, he could put me out of business if he could only pass on his philosophies to the rest of the world.

However, the man I liked most, in my recent acquaintances, was Brad Manchester. Jane had introduced us and he hardly left her side. I'd met with a lot of lawyers. In my line of business they came with the territory. And I knew, in very short order, that Brad was one of the good ones. Jane had told me about the Maplewood case. About the divorced woman's fight to protect her son, and their subsequent win in court the previous month.

And waiting outside the courtroom I'd heard Brad speaking with Sheila about a couple of cases, as well.

His questions and later answers had been sharp, insightful.

Yeah, Brad was obviously a good lawyer. Still, there was a guy who could use a head butting.

Of course, if I'd ever met anyone even remotely like him, I'd be sharing my life with someone who weighed more than four pounds.

I mean, Camelia was great company, but every once in a while—okay, often—I yearned to be held. To be touched...

But that was enough about me. Jane had just been called to the stand and sworn in again for the record as this was a new trial. New charges, too. Along with murder, Shelia had been able to win a grand jury indictment for assault against Jane. The judge had agreed to hear both cases together.

Within minutes I knew that my patient didn't need me anymore.

THE COURT CALLED A RECESS as Jane stepped down from the stand to join Brad in the gallery of the courtroom. James didn't move from his seat at the defendant's table but raised his voice to be sure she'd hear him.

"You've changed."

Jane didn't look at him. But she saw his lawyer grab his arm and engage him in low-voiced, but obviously intense, conversation.

Sanders Elliot had shown great skill in rehabilitating his client's testimony. Hopefully this time his best effort wouldn't be good enough.

"I SAW MARLA ANDERSON."

Brad had been keeping a vigilant eye on Jane all afternoon and was glad to have her safely ensconced in her seat for the flight home. He'd thought she was sleeping.

"The athletic-looking blonde?" They hadn't stayed for any of the rest of the trial, but he'd seen the woman, who'd been sitting in the front row, exchange glances with James Todd.

"Yeah."

"What did you think of her?"

"That, for all of her money and success, she's as needy as James is. Or as manipulated by him as I was."

"She's seen Dr. Chapman, too, hasn't she?"

"Yes. I can only hope Kelly can help her as much as she's helped me."

"I guess that's up to Ms. Anderson, though, isn't it?"

A person could only be helped if he was willing to help himself. That's what the psychologist had told Brad when he'd thanked her for what she'd done for Jane.

"I guess." She closed her eyes again.

"What did you think of James?" Jane asked a couple of minutes later.

"That he's a bit too sure of himself and eventually he's going to come in contact with someone who won't fall for his lies."

"But they aren't all lies," Jane said. "That's what makes it so damaging—and so hard to see. James really does care about a lot of things. He was passionate about his work. He cared about me at first, and probably Lee Anne, too. Problem is, he cares desperately, which drives his need to control."

Brad understood all of that. He just didn't give a damn about the man's heart or his needs.

What he cared about, deep down, he'd never admit to Jane. He cared about her. And he cared about the fact that he could never, ever, risk hurting her. She'd been hurt enough.

JANE WAS ALONE in her office just after five on Monday, looking at lists of baby names on the Internet, when she got the call.

"Boss, it's Sam."

She'd been waiting for her head writer to check in with her from the trial. The jury had been out for hours.

"And?"

"Guilty on all counts of assault. For both you and Lee Anne. Not guilty of murder. I'm so sorry. There just wasn't enough evidence to prove that Lee Anne didn't commit suicide.

"That Elliot swine brought in an expert on abused women this morning, changing the defense from simply that of a depressed woman to that of an abused woman. Basically, they chose to take a chance on the less serious charges to beat the murder charge. Their expert showed documentation proving that women who've been abused are five times more likely to commit suicide, which, in addition to the antidepressants and the lack of conclusive physical proof, put enough doubt in the jurors' minds to get him off. I think his lawyer told him that selling him up the river on the abuse, using that to strengthen Lee Anne's supposed suicidal state, was the only way to get him off the murder charges. There just wasn't enough evidence to prove that he was actually with Lee Anne when she fell."

Because James knew how to make "accidents." No evidence of criminal activity.

He'd killed Lee Anne. Jane had been sure of that since the trial, for no other reason than that she'd finally looked at James with her eyes wide open. And she'd seen what he really was.

"So he faces six felony convictions?" Lee Anne's

sister had only been able to provide enough evidence for Sheila to get the grand jury to indict him on two counts of abuse for the dead woman.

"And two misdemeanors with aggravators for the bigamy charges."

"When's sentencing?"

"Next month."

Jane would have to testify again then. Sheila had already told her that. And without the murder conviction, the hearing would just be held before the judge. Not a jury.

"So he's free until then?"

"No." Sam's voice took on a much lighter note. "Because of his treatment of you, both in the past and more recently, the judge ordered him into custody until the hearing. Each felony conviction comes with a maximum sentence of five years and I gotta tell you, boss, I'm getting the feeling that this guy's going away for a while."

So James hadn't won after all.

BRAD WAS IN COURT when Jane's call came through. She told him the news over voice mail and didn't pick up when he called her back.

Not sure if she was avoiding him or if she was just busy, he left a message congratulating her profusely and hung up.

At least the bastard was in jail. That in itself was a huge relief.

His own relationship with Jane, however, continued to cause him intense discomfort. He loved her. But was love enough? He'd thought he loved Emily, too, though certainly not with the mind-destroying intensity of his feelings for Jane.

When, in his car on the way home at the end of the day, Brad couldn't face the idea of another evening alone with his thoughts, he scrolled through his contacts and hit dial.

"Hey, Em, how you doing?" He spoke into his Bluetooth as she picked up.

"Brad? Hi! What's up?"

"You got a minute?"

"Ten, actually. I've just finished up at school, and I'm on my way to pick up J.J. at day care."

J.J. Jeff Junior. Emily's three-year-old son. Emily and Jeff's. "How's Junior doing?"

"Great. Oh, Brad, he's grown so much since you saw him." Brad had run into the small family just after Junior's first birthday. He'd been in the city, on his way to meet Jane at her office to take her to dinner. Emily and Jeff had just come across the street from the lake. It was the first time Brad had seen Emily since she'd had her baby. She'd seemed so different, so peaceful. He'd been thrilled for her.

Now he felt envious.

He'd seen Emily and Jeff since. But he'd never seen the baby again.

"For such a little guy, he talks constantly," Emily was saying and Brad made certain he heard every word. "He has all these theories that crack us up, but, of course, we don't let him know that. He says that on his next birthday he's going to turn twenty so he can be old and go to the moon."

Motherhood suited her. Would he be half as good a parent to his own baby?

"And Jeff?"

"He's fine, too. Just got another promotion. He's director of IT now."

Jeff Miller, a computer whiz from one of Chicago's business conglomerates whom Emily had met while taking her high school seniors on a tour of his company, seemed genuinely devoted to Brad's ex-wife.

"Good for him," Brad said sincerely. "Tell him congratulations for me."

"I will."

"And what about you? Is the semester going well?" Emily taught math and computer science in the Chicago suburb where she and Jeff lived.

"Things are a little crazy right now," she said, but didn't sound the least bit put out by it. "You know how it gets in the spring with graduation looming just over the horizon."

He remembered a spring night when Emily had come home from school bubbling with all of the plans her senior students had for their futures. And how upset she'd been when she'd realized he hadn't heard a word.

He hadn't meant to zone out on her. Hadn't even realized he had until he'd noticed the tears. When had her voice become soporific to him? Something that lulled him into mental meanderings rather than engaging him?

"I remember," he said now, gazing at the front door of his house. He'd pulled into his driveway, but didn't get out of the car. "Listen, Em, I just wanted to ask, to make sure…you're happy now, aren't you?"

Please, God, let the guilt fade into the dark, dusty corners of his life, no longer a constant weight on his shoulders.

"Yeah! Of course I am. Why do you ask?"

She had to be close to the day care by now.

"I…" He wondered what good could really be served by rehashing things best left alone. And then he thought of Jane and her inability to trust her judgment when it came to relationships. She couldn't afford another selfish man in her life. "I need to ask you something," he said now, picturing Emily's sweet face puckered into a frown. An attentive look her students would recognize.

"I'm listening."

"If we were still married, do you think you'd be as happy as you are today?"

The pause on the line was tough to take.

"I don't know how to answer that."

Brad sighed. "Honestly, please. It's really important, Em, or I wouldn't have asked."

"I...don't want to hurt you."

That was rich. And so typical of Emily to worry about his feelings even after he'd broken her heart so many times.

"Please, I need to know."

"No, Brad, I wouldn't be as happy as I am now."

His ego was bruised, and yet Brad was relieved, too. Incredibly relieved. He'd treated her badly, but in the end, maybe he'd done her a favor, too.

If nothing else, at least the damage he'd done hadn't ruined her whole life.

"Jeff is absolutely the one for me," Emily continued, her voice soft. "What I feel for him is so much deeper, so much more, than I ever felt for you."

All right, already. But it was exactly what he'd had to know.

"So when you thought you were head over heels in love with me, you were wrong?"

She'd been so certain when they got married that he was it. She'd told him so. Written the words in cards, in letters and put them in her wedding vows.

"No..." Her response came more slowly this time. "I

was completely in love with you. But it takes a mutual love, a mutual vulnerability to each other, to take 'in love' to the deeper level. I was never sure of your love, Brad, and that stifled my own. I wanted to give you my whole heart, but I don't think you'd have known what to do with it."

Making divorce more a matter of lack of commitment, than lack of love?

"Would you?" Emily's question made him blink.

"No, probably not," he was ashamed to say. "I'm sorry, Em. So, so sorry."

"You don't think I know that?" Her response took him by surprise. "You're a good man, Brad, and a very kind one. Which is part of the reason we got into the mess we did. You were afraid to tell me that you didn't love me as much as I loved you."

"I thought I did." For a very short time. And then he'd stood by his promise to her.

"Besides," she added. "The fault wasn't all yours. I could have left and I didn't. I knew you weren't happy but I chose to hold you, anyway. I was thinking of me, not you."

"If you had it to do over again, would you have left?"

"Absolutely. Maybe I'd have found Jeff sooner. And if nothing else, it would have put us both out of our misery more quickly."

"Our misery?"

"You think I don't know how guilty you feel about us, even now? You think I didn't see that same guilt in your eyes every time I told you how much I loved you and you'd tell me you loved me, too?"

More than ten minutes had passed. She must be parked at the day care, the same way he was at home.

"I had no idea. I'm so damned sorry."

"Hey, if not for you, I might not appreciate what I have with Jeff so much. I learned a lot about relationships from our marriage, Brad. I learned what I need, and what it takes to make it work."

Emily's tone was light and the words made him think. Was he completely missing the boat here? Instead of letting his experience with Emily scare him off, did he, instead, have the tools to make his next relationship last forever?

"So tell me, Brad, what brought all this on today? You said my answer was important. Why?"

The question jarred him out of his thoughts. Same old Emily, wanting to jump right into his skin.

And if it were Jane who wanted to be there?

"Jane and I..."

He told her about getting his friend pregnant, leaving out the details. About how crazy he'd been ever since, thinking about Jane all the time.

"You've changed."

"I've finally come to terms with myself," he said, their history allowing him to be more frank than he was with anyone. Except Jane.

"I wanted it easy," Brad continued before he could change his mind. Emily deserved to hear this. "When I married you—and afterward—I wanted everything. I wanted it perfect. *And* I wanted a guarantee that I wasn't ever going to be hurt."

It hadn't really been about loving or not loving Emily at all.

"Wow, you *have* changed. I'm impressed." The smile in her voice touched a chord of deep fondness within him. He truly had cared about his ex-wife. "And I'm glad," she said. "You deserve to be happy."

"Don't be too impressed," he cautioned. "I didn't just reach these conclusions on my own." He'd been pushed by a woman who didn't like him all that much, if he had his guess. Kelly Chapman had never had him as a patient, had never had more than a brief passing conversation with him, but she'd changed his life with one line.

A person can only be helped if he's willing to help himself.

She'd ostensibly been talking about Jane, but Brad had a feeling the truism had been directed at him.

He'd put himself on the stand, questioned himself— bringing him some of the most uncomfortable moments of his life.

"So where have these revelations led you?" Emily asked as Brad stared at a smudge in the middle of his garage door.

"I've been a fraud." Jane's earlier words. But they hadn't described her. "Thinking I'm going along without a care in the world. When in truth, I love Jane Hamilton—probably have from the beginning. And I'm petrified of failure."

"And where does that lead you?" she asked.

"I haven't figured that part out yet."

But he would. Of that Brad was certain.

"JANE, I HAVE ONE HERE you might want to read." Marge entered Jane's office door the first Tuesday in August with a printed page in her hand.

Jane's stomach dropped and her heart started to pound. Not again. She'd finally given up her extra protection a couple of weeks after the verdict. Driver and all.

James was in jail. His mail would be monitored....

"Oh, I'm so sorry, don't worry." Marge came closer, her words tripping over themselves. "It's an editorial that just came in for the August issue."

"It's too late to add anything else." Leftover anxiety made her terse.

"I know, but I think you might want to hold the presses for this one."

Curious about Marge's unusual enthusiasm for a reader letter, Jane took the page from her. Marge kept the envelope from which it had obviously come.

With one last glance at her editor, Jane started to read. Her throat caught at the title.

Loving an Abused Woman.
Dear Jane,
I am not a woman, nor a regular reader of your magazine. I am acquainted with a woman you have helped. You opened her eyes and she sought help. There is no way I can thank you, but I wanted to tell you what I've learned about loving a woman who's been abused in case it can be of benefit to someone else.
1. *Love is about self-sacrifice. It's not about her sacrifice. Don't measure what you give by how much she gives you.*

Jane's eyes filled with tears, blurring her vision. She read through them.

2. *Make certain that you have the courage to love her if she's afraid to love you back. That you have the courage to love her even if she doesn't love you back.*
3. *Believe her when she says she doesn't trust*

*herself. Believe her and help her even though
you might not understand. She is fighting internal demons that you will never know.*

4. *Be there for her even in those times when she's
lost in darkness and you feel useless. Those are
the times she needs you most.*

5. *Accept that you're paying for the sins of another man. She is, too. And her price was far
higher than yours.*

6. *If you are lucky enough to be wanted by her,
you will be loved more intensely, more faith-
fully, more completely than you could ever
imagine because this is a woman who's been
to the wall and doesn't play games with her
heart or anyone else's. Be grateful that she's
chosen to take a chance on you.*

The letter ended there, with no signature.

Jane reached for a tissue, and then, when she could,
asked Marge, "Who sent this?"

Marge didn't speak as she handed the envelope to
Jane. The return address was written in a familiar bold
script.

Brad Manchester.

JANE INVITED BRAD to go hiking on Saturday. He'd
expected more of a walk in the park, given the fact that
she was beginning to look as though she was carrying around a bowling ball under her shirt. Instead, she
directed him to the same trail he'd chosen that day in
March when he'd done the unthinkable.

"Let me get that," he said when she pulled out the
backpack she'd thrown in his trunk.

"That's okay, I've got it." Hooking the straps over her

shoulders, she buckled a water bottle around her hips, beneath her belly. The denim shorts, which he knew bore a full stretch panel because he'd purchased them for her, with a pink top, pink socks and tennis shoes should have been ordinary, but Brad had to catch his breath.

Jane made pregnant look like art.

She led the way for a while. And then he did—keeping the pace easy and slow. They talked about the plants, the picnic he'd packed and was carrying. How she'd slept the night before. She never mentioned the letter to the editor he'd sent to *Twenty-Something*. Since he had no way of knowing if she'd even seen it, he didn't mention it, either.

When they reached the summit Jane plopped down on the same fallen log she'd sat on the last time they'd been there and Brad was struck with a sudden sense of foreboding.

"Oh!" Jane jumped and Brad looked for her to brush a bug off her leg or her neck. "Come here," she said instead, her hand on her belly.

Concerned, he sat beside her, allowing her to take his hand. Placing it on her belly, she said, "Wait."

He waited. And then…he felt it. The slightest fluttering. Not a kick. Nothing like a kick. More like tiny bubbles hitting her skin from the inside out.

Brad stared at his hand. And then at her. "It's alive," he said, inanely.

Chuckling, Jane pressed his hand against her. "Wait. There'll probably be more. I felt it the first time this week. At first, I thought it was just gas."

"Is that what it feels like?" He wasn't sure what to do with his hand on her stomach. Taking it away didn't seem to be an option.

"Mostly. Just like air bubbles moving around in there."

The baby moved again and he was a goner. Successful lawyer, man's man, eligible bachelor be damned. He was going to be a daddy.

"Now seems like a good time to take care of something else," Jane said, letting go of his hand while she slipped out of her backpack. Pulling a large, slightly rumpled gift bag from it, she handed it to him.

"For me?" he asked, taking it. "What's the occasion?"

"Just open it and then we'll talk."

Curious and slightly apprehensive, Brad dug down into the tissue. His mixed emotions didn't diminish as he found what it concealed. A very worn Raggedy Ann doll, folded at the waist. The stuffed toy's black cloth feet and red-and-white-striped legs dangled as Brad held her up. Her face, also cloth with painted-on nose and mouth and black plastic button eyes, was filthy. Streaks and smears covered her cheeks, almost as though she'd been crying.

He didn't get it. Didn't know what to say. Obviously something important was happening. Brad had never felt more like a guy than he did in that moment, sitting with his pregnant whatever she was, holding a doll.

"I've had her, or a version of her, since I was a little girl." Jane's words saved him from hurting her by revealing his inadequate comprehension. Inadequate appreciation. Or emotional intuitiveness. "My dad gave me my first Raggy when I was three. He was on his way to Germany for two years. Of course, at the time, I had no idea what that meant. That doll was bigger than I was. He told me when I needed to give him a hug, she'd be his stand-in."

There might have been a breeze. Brad felt as though the world had stopped spinning.

"I slept with that doll until she was so frayed she could no longer be fixed. I was a teenager by then. I came home from school the day after we'd decided to throw her away, and found a brand-new Raggy waiting on my bed for me. She was smaller, but perfect."

"Your mother bought her?"

"Nope. My stepdad did."

He was beginning to see a pattern here. Something about the good men in her life, the ones who made her feel safe. He hoped he was one of them.

"Is this her?"

Jane shook her head. "James spilled a can of paint on her."

Another "accident," Brad supposed.

Looking at the doll, she rubbed her hands together almost as though she didn't know what to do with them. He was tempted to hand the doll back to her, but didn't.

"I bought that one," she said. "The first time James hurt me. I hid her from him. And any night he wasn't at home, I slept with her."

Her eyes were moist as she looked at Brad. "And every night since I left him, I've slept with her. Except when I travel. Every single night."

He thought he was starting to understand. Maybe.

"How'd she get so dirty?" He traced the smudges on the cloth cheeks.

"Mascara marks." She tried to blow off the comment with a smirk that didn't quite make it. "Tears."

He had to ask. "Why are you giving her to me?"

"Two reasons," Jane said. When she took hold of an edge of the doll's dress he saw how badly her hands were trembling. "First, because I don't need her anymore. She took the place of the man in my life, she comforted me, kept me safe."

Now he was afraid to ask. "And why don't you need her anymore?"

"Because I have you. You're the best friend I've ever had. The best champion I've ever had."

Brad didn't realize he was scrunching the doll in his hands until he saw her skewed features through blurry eyes.

Would this amazing woman ever stop surprising him? *Please, God, don't let me let her down. Give me the strength and the know-how to be there for her. Always.*

"Do you want to know the second reason?" Jane's voice broke.

Brad nodded.

He was a little taken aback when Jane pushed up the bottom of the doll's dress, seemingly undressing her.

"See that?"

She exposed a red heart, painted on the left side of the doll's chest. Inscribed inside were the words *I Love You.*

"As long as I had Raggy's love, I was okay," she said. "I didn't need anyone else. Now I do. Now I'm giving myself—and her—to you."

Brad's heart was so full, he didn't think he could take any more. Until Jane said, "You need her now. She's there for you to hold anytime you start to feel guilty. Or to be afraid that you can't love enough. Because over the past two years her heart has become a symbol to me of yours."

He didn't even bother to try to hide the tears in his

eyes. Life had just become all that he'd ever imagined. And far more.

"There's one more thing," Jane said.

There was nothing else she could give him that would matter. He already had it all.

"In her pocket." She pointed to the little ruffled pocket on the front of Raggedy Ann's white apron.

He could only fit two fingers inside. He only needed one. Hooking the ring around his finger, he pulled it out.

"I figure since I've already rejected you twice, it might be a really long time before you ask again, so, Brad Manchester, will you marry me?"

Brad stared at the thick, gold band.

And hoped there was a smaller band to go with it. He wanted his ring on her finger.

But first things first. There was one thing Brad knew he was good at. That they were great at. He pulled Jane into his arms, and spent the rest of the afternoon lovingly, gently and oh, so reverently accepting her proposal.

* * * * *

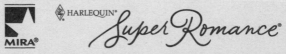

HARLEQUIN® *SuperRomance*®

COMING NEXT MONTH

Available October 12, 2010

#1662 THE GOOD PROVIDER
Spotlight on Sentinel Pass
Debra Salonen

#1663 THE SCANDAL AND CARTER O'NEILL
The Notorious O'Neills
Molly O'Keefe

#1664 ADOPTED PARENTS
Suddenly a Parent
Candy Halliday

#1665 CALLING THE SHOTS
You, Me & the Kids
Ellen Hartman

#1666 THAT RUNAWAY SUMMER
Return to Indigo Springs
Darlene Gardner

#1667 DANCE WITH THE DOCTOR
Single Father
Cindi Myers

MIRA®

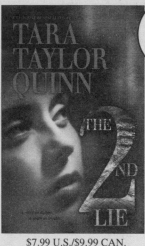

$7.99 U.S./$9.99 CAN.

Look for the next book in *The Chapman Files* series from *USA TODAY* bestselling author

TARA TAYLOR QUINN

THE SECOND LIE

Available September 28, 2010, wherever books are sold!

✂

$1.00 OFF the purchase price of THE SECOND LIE by Tara Taylor Quinn

Offer valid from September 28, 2010, to October 12, 2010.
Redeemable at participating retail outlets. Limit one coupon per purchase.
Valid in the U.S.A. and Canada only.

You've Just read THE FIRST WIFE
by *USA TODAY* bestselling author

TARA TAYLOR QUINN

Continue to follow psychologist Kelly Chapman with
the next three books in *The Chapman Files* series.

October

November

December

AVAILABLE WHEREVER
BOOKS ARE SOLD!

MIRA®

MTTQIBC

ISBN-13:978-0-373-71656-2

Jane's rule about marriage: if at first you don't succeed, **don't** *try again*

A bigamist ex-husband, an anonymous stalker, a murder inquiry. Magazine editor Jane Hamilton is *not* having a good month. But with the support of her best friend, Brad Manchester, she's coping—until they become lovers and Brad complicates things even more by proposing marriage.

Brad understands Jane's fears, but he's ready for a wife and family, ready to move forward. Especially when he finds out she's pregnant with *his* child.

THE NEXT BOOKS WITH KELLY CHAPMAN

$5.50 U.S./$6.50 CAN.
ISBN-13:978-0-373-71656-2

50550

9 780373 716562

EAN

HEART & HOME

Harlequin® SuperRomance®
www.eHarlequin.com